SMOKY JOE'S CAFE

Bryce Courtenay is the bestselling author of *The Power of One*, *Tandia*, *The Potato Factory*, *Tommo & Hawk*, *Jessica*, *Solomon's Song*, *The Australian Trilogy*, *The Night Country* and *Smoky Joe's Cafe*. He was born in South Africa, is an Australian and has lived in Sydney for the major part of his life.

Further information about the
author may be found at
www.brycecourtenay.com

McArthur & Company
Toronto

BRYCE COURTENAY

McArthur & Company

Toronto

First Published in Canada by McArthur & Company, 2001

First Canadian Paperback Edition Published by McArthur & Company, 2002

McArthur & Company
322 King St. West
Suite 402
Toronto, Ontario
M5V 1J2

An earlier, shorter version of this story was first published electronically as *Meeting at the Smoky Joe Cafe, 2000*

National Library of Canada Cataloguing in Publication

Courtenay, Bryce, 1933-
    Smoky Joe's Cafe / Bryce Courtenay.

ISBN 1-55278-304-9

    I. Title.

PR9619.3.C598S56 2002   823   C2002-903009-9

Design by Cathy Larsen
Printed in Canada by Transcontinental Printing Inc.

The Publisher would like to acknowledge the financial support of the Government of Canada through the Book Publishing Industry Development Program (BPIDP) and the Canada Council for our publishing activities.

10 9 8 7 6 5 4 3 2 1

*To the men of 11 Platoon, D Company, 6 RAR,
those who are alive and those who gave their lives
at the Battle of Long Tan.*

*Also, to the combined Australian Forces
who served in Vietnam.*

'Weapons Training' by Bruce Dawe on pages 68–69, from *Condolences of the Season*, is reproduced by permission of Pearson Education Australia.

ACKNOWLEDGEMENTS

The Australian experience in the Vietnam war was very different to that of the American one and so this book has been a very personal journey for me, an intellectual fact-finding tour that leaves me extremely proud of the way our boys accomplished a difficult and controversial job in Vietnam.

Vietnam was a very different kind of war and one we probably shouldn't have been involved in. Be that as it may, our nation's reluctant acceptance as worthy warriors of the young men who returned from Vietnam simply wasn't justified. A revision of our negative attitude towards their Vietnam experience is long overdue.

I hope you enjoy the story, which, of course, is a work of fiction. My eleven platoon characters are also wholly fictional and do not in any way portray any of the infantrymen who fought at Long Tan and who remain alive. However, the effort undertaken to portray the Vietnam experience is as close to the truth as, I believe, diligent research could make it.

A great many people need to be thanked for their help in getting the hard facts right and in sharing their experiences for my benefit. First among these is Celia Jarvis, who accomplished a remarkable amount of research in a short time and did so with admirable patience and good humour. My special thanks to Graham Walker, a Vietnam veteran himself, for his counsel and guidance throughout.

Others, in alphabetical order, who were generous with

information and who gave their permission to use their own Vietnam experiences, written or otherwise, are Bob Buick MM, Wayne Cowan, Rod Cozins, Owen Denmeade, Peter James, Terry Loftus, Tim McCoomb, Mike McDermitt, Gary McMahon, Ross Mangano, Ern Marshall, Stanley Morrie MBE, Harry Smith MC, Keith White, Tony White, Barry Wright and Admiral E.R. Zumwalt Jnr.

I especially thank the Granville office in Sydney of the Vietnam Veterans Federation who were enormously helpful in organising for me to interview a number of veterans, all of whom I thank for speaking so candidly about their post-Vietnam experience. Also, the Vietnam Veterans Association of Australia for making available various papers and submissions to the government on the effects of Agent Orange and other veteran health issues.

For the marijuana/cannabis information, my thanks go to Robert Long of the Nimbin Hemp Embassy and to the authors of various websites on the Internet. For the information on bone-marrow transplants, I am grateful to the Prince of Wales Hospital, Randwick, Sydney.

I also thank those authors who have gone before me and who have written so well on the Vietnam war. Bob Buick and Gary McKay, *All Guts and No Glory*; Terry Burstall, *The Soldier's Story*; Lex McAulay, *The Battle of Long Tan*; Ian McNeill, *To Long Tan, The Australian Army and the Vietnam*

War 1950–1966; and Captain Nick Welsh, *A History of the Sixth Battalion, The Royal Australian Regiment 1965–85*.

All that remains is to thank Robert Sessions, my publisher at Penguin Books, and my editor, Kay Ronai, who, realising this was a difficult story for me to write, helped more than I can say.

Chapter One

Nightmares, don't tell me about them. Every night as it begins to grow dark I open a bottle of Scotch. I tell myself, if I can get pissed enough they won't come. I'll be so motherless, so brain dead by the time I crawl into the misery of sleep that my subconscious will leave me alone, let me get through the night without the terror.

It works sometimes, but not often enough. It's the night noises; I wake to a noise, any noise, and the anxiety builds. Before I know it, I'm up with the knife and on patrol around our living quarters upstairs, then downstairs to the cafe, then into the backyard and the storage shed, I even check the pavement outside Smoky Joe's before I come back to bed and lie awake shaking like a sheila. I sleep with a Confederate Bowie, a real bastard of a knife, a copy of the standard army issue used by the Confederate troops in the American Civil War.

I took it off a Yank Marine at Vung Tau. He was so pissed he could hardly stand up and he reckoned he'd been dudded by a bar girl and it looked like he was about to use it on her. I grabbed his arm and took the knife just as the provosts, the military police, arrived. They took him away and I still had the knife. I reckoned I'd earned it anyway. The little whore lost no time demonstrating how grateful she was to me neither.

The Confederate has an eleven-inch blade forged from Damascus steel, it lies safe under my pillow where I can get to it fast. If the bastards come for me I'm ready. Wendy has begged me to throw it away. She's terrified I'll wake up screaming, like I've done a hundred times already, and use it before I'm truly awake. On her, me, the kid.

More than once I've wrecked the joint before I've woke up properly. Or I've grabbed her and covered her with my body screaming, 'Hold on, Mo, the dustoff's coming, you're gunna be okay! Hold on, please, Mo, I love you, mate! Don't fucking die on me, you bastard!' Looking down at Wendy, Nog AK47s going off, *crackle-pop-crackle-pop-pop-pop*, our machine gun, *brrrrrrrr-bam-bam-bam*, the noise all about me, grunts shouting, firing every which way, the noise of the dustoff blades *putta-putta-putta-putta* as the helicopter comes in to pick up the wounded, her head is missing, blood everywhere. Wendy's head is Mo's head and then it switches around again. But in the nightmare I tell myself, 'How can me mate live with no head?'

So here I am, a screwed-up Vietnam veteran. No better or worse than my mates and not quite knowing what's gone wrong. Flashbacks, nightmares, rage, dizzy spells, anxiety, paranoia, insomnia, depression, sometimes long periods of impotence, and a whole heap more, that's me. Bloody pathetic, isn't it?

The quacks at Repat shake their heads, say they've done all the tests and nothing shows up. Veterans Affairs, taking directions from Canberra, who, taking their brief straight from the Pentagon, simply repeat the official line. One bloke who interviews me has this half smile on his face, 'Mr Thompson, as far as the department is concerned your psychological problems are not caused by your war experience. You have been diagnosed with a personality disorder. Maybe it was something that happened in your childhood, something your mother or father did to you. And as far as Agent Orange is concerned it's about as harmless to humans as baby powder.'

Baby powder? Now that's real funny, but the bastard doesn't know it.

Once, we'd been out in the jungle for three weeks and we know exactly where we are, we've just used a smoke grenade and a passing chopper has radioed in to give us an accurate location. So we know from looking at the map that there's a lot more deep j ahead, at least four days of scrub bashing before the operation is over.

Then suddenly a couple of hours further into the boonies and it's not there, the jungle's missing, a miracle. Instead of visibility of maybe six yards we can see ahead of us for five hundred yards. Everything in front of us is dead and we're kicking up this fine white powder. Touch a dead tree and the dust comes down to cover your greens, smells weird too. (Unbeknownst to our intelligence, the Yanks had defoliated the area two weeks previously.) What was supposed to be in the middle of primary rainforest is like a dead world.

This was the first time I'd seen what Agent Orange could do, though, of course, I had no idea at the time what it was, or how the dense jungle came to be defoliated. Let me tell you, there was nothing left alive. We saw dead bats, birds, spiders, every kind of insect you could imagine and not a green leaf on anything, everything silent, all of it covered with this fine white powder that looked just like baby powder.

I'd have liked to have told the arsehole in Vets Affairs that story but he wouldn't have listened anyway, they're experts at nodding your life into non-existence.

In Vietnam we fought with the Yanks, though not alongside them. A lot of them were half stoned most of the time, which we soon learned wasn't an addiction but a bloody necessity. At their Blackhorse Base in Long Khanh province, the US Army divided their platoons into potheads and non-potheads. The potheads did the day work and the non-potheads the night work. Though not the Marines, Airborne and Special Forces, the professional soldiers, they stayed clean and as warriors they don't come a lot better.

If the Yank conscripts had stayed off Mary Jane, their name for dope, I reckon there'd be a lot less names carved on that granite wall they've got in Washington.

We used grog not dope for the same purpose. Frankly, you needed something just to get the jungle and the fear out of your head for a while. You couldn't go into the jungle half stoned, gung-ho, thinking you were John Wayne, and hope to stay alive. No way, grog or dope was always for afterwards.

There's another point I should make here in case

you think I'm knocking the Yanks. The kids they sent to Vietnam were like eighteen years old, just out of high school, they were still boys. The youngest of our Australian conscripts were closer to twenty-one. Those three or four years make a bloody big difference in a bloke's life. Then there's the training. Compared with us, your average Yank recruit hadn't even received the basic instruction for survival in jungle warfare.

The Noggies or Nogs, they were the two names we used mostly for the Viet Cong, other names were Charlie, Cong, VC and NVA, they used weed too. But, like the Australians, not when they were fighting. Without the help of one substance or another, I count grog as one of them, the warriors on both sides would have laid down their AK47s, SLRs, M16s or Owen guns and gone home to their wives or girlfriends.

That was the whole point of Vietnam, us and the Nogs were shitting ourselves every time we went into the jungle. I once heard a black American sergeant explain what it was like in Vietnam, 'Your asshole's turned inside out like permanent, man!'

The bloody jungle was the enemy as much as the Viet Cong. Sometimes it was dense with a tall canopy of big trees, like the rainforest in New Guinea, or up North, which wasn't hard to work. But in areas where it had been bombed it became secondary growth with lots of bamboo everywhere, all of it tangled and dense and bloody hard to see into or move through. Or when you fought around the river, the mangrove forests were like a jungle. That is, before the Yanks come up with their big idea.

There wasn't only Agent Orange, but Agent Blue, Green, Purple, White, you name it, they had a colour for everything and every colour killed something. They sprayed this shit over the jungle like the monsoon rains had come early. Only this time the clouds were coming from the helicopters and the C123s fitted with spraying arms that swarmed over the jungle like huge insects pissing down on the trees.

At the time nobody really asked if it was dangerous, we all reckoned if they were spraying this stuff where we were fighting and even living it couldn't be harmful to us. Nobody in their right mind would put their own troops in danger, would they?

The Hygiene Unit at Nui Dat sprayed insecticides like DDT, Malathion and Dieldrin round the camp on anything that moved. They sprayed it in our tents, in our weapon pits, in our kitchens and mess halls and in our latrines. It would be on the plates we ate off and the cups we drank from. It's so toxic, Dieldrin is now banned in every country in the world because it's a carcinogenic and deadly to humans.

That's just one of dozens of chemicals used. Of course, we were told the stuff they sprayed everywhere was deadly to insects, leaves, rice paddies, rivers, mozzies, spiders, in fact to everything that grew or breathed except humans.

I guess when you're twenty-one years old you'll believe just about anything the army tells you. And, if it isn't quite the whole truth, well, what the hell, they just kept denying everything. She'll be right, no worries, trust me, son.

'Mr Thompson,' the quack from Veterans Affairs said, 'it's probably a slight blood disorder, perfectly natural in some people, the severe acne, it will clear up in time, I should think.'

I remember how he examined the lesions on my cheeks, behind the ears, under the armpits and into my groin, deep cysts and acne, blackheads the size of your pinkie nail. 'Hmm, interesting,' is all he said. I showed him how my palms were sweating all the time and took off my shoes and showed him my sweating feet and the peculiar smell that came from them. I pointed to the sores and blisters on the back of my hands.

He looks at my hands, he's wearing these thin plastic

gloves so he don't have to touch me. 'It says here you're a mechanic by trade, Mr Thompson.' He looks up from the form in front of him, 'It just could be something you've picked up in the mechanic's workshop, probably battery acid.'

Battery acid! Doesn't he know I'd know if I'd spilt battery acid over the back of me hands?

'I'll take the precaution and give you a note to the Shire Health Inspector,' he says and starts to write as he continues talking. 'As for your insomnia and anxiety, it's perfectly natural, an adjustment to civilian life. I'll give you a prescription.' What the bastard was really saying was, 'You Vietnam vets oughta pull yerself together.' That's my interpretation, that he thinks we're a bunch of wimps and to go home and get on with our lives with the help of a cocktail made up of Moggies, Valium and Scotch.

But I digress. I am aware that Vietnam is forgotten history, a sort of national disgrace we've swept under the political-conscience carpet. It was a war where Bob Menzies, who was Prime Minister of Australia at the time and therefore father of the nation, reckoned a bit of a stoush would do our lads the world of good, make real men out of us. Well, if those weren't exactly his words, it's the same difference. He thought it would be good for Australia, good for the national character, or a similar piece of total and utter bullshit.

So, for the moment, if you'll forgive the impertinence to Menzies and Holt, who followed him, let me talk about those who were regular army and those, like me, whose names got pulled out of the barrel to go to Vietnam on behalf of the national character and our undying friendship with the U.S. of A.

We were the blokes who returned from Vietnam to find that the national character now required that we be treated like a bunch of mercenaries guilty of war crimes. It seems the real heroes were the nice little boys and girls who marched in the Anti-Vietnam rallies chanting slogans, waving the Viet Cong flag and passing a joint around while the cops looked on. We came back to an Australia where smoking dope was fashionable among the young trendies, who thought of themselves as weekend hippies and after-hours flower children.

The church, as usual, switched sides, with the Vietnam moratoriums specked with back-to-front collars. Then, of course, there were the trade unions, urged on by the Labor left, who had their digit finger severely up their bums trying to make a stink in Canberra.

Well, back home again I soon enough find out that I can't work for any bastard, not even as a builder's labourer. I'm a qualified, three-certificate mechanic by trade, GM, Ford and Datsun, passed all the courses as well as topped my tech course. I'm aware I'm no Einstein, but I'm not exactly a bird brain neither. But I can't get under a car without going into a blind panic. I try to keep my nose clean as a labourer, but soon enough the building foreman looks at me the wrong way, or in my fevered brain I think he does, and next thing I've got a fistful of his overalls and his gumboots are a foot off the ground. Being a real big bloke with the post-Vietnam blues is not a likeable combination and I'm beginning to hate myself more even than I hate the civilian world I've come back into.

When I first came back I tried running a service station, took over the BP franchise in the small town where I was born in the Riverina. My folk have been here for four generations, long before the irrigation canal. My great-grandfather and his brother Jim came up overland by wagon from Sydney and they started up a blacksmith shop. Jim, it seemed, was a bit fond of the bottle and took up with an Aboriginal gin and went walkabout. Anyway he disappeared from the Thompson family history never to be heard of again. My great-grandfather died working at the anvil and my grandfather took over from him and did the selfsame, died with the blast furnace at his back and a hammer in his hand. If they went to hell the devil would've handed them a hammer each and they'd have carried on like nothing had happened. Then my old man turned the smithy into Thompson's Garage, the first petrol pump in town. There have been Thompsons in Currawong Creek since before they dug the first dunny.

Well, eventually the old man, carrying on the family tradition, dropped dead while pumping petrol. This was while I was away in Vietnam. BP took over the site and developed it into a state-of-the-art service station just about the time I got back.

I come back a bit of a war hero, well in Currawong Creek anyway, where there didn't seem to be any anti-Vietnam backlash, which says something for the town at least. The Bank of New South Wales give me a loan. 'Always been a Thompson running things mechanical in this town,' the manager says, dead chuffed with himself as I sign my flamin' life away as the local BP franchisee.

Green and yellow are the BP corporate colours, the colour of the jungle and my own cowardice. Not a very promising start in the service station business with me shitting myself every time I crawl under a ute. Being a BP dealer doesn't last long. Any skills I may have previously possessed in public relations I shat into my greens fighting the Noggies in a rubber plantation at Long Tan. Sure enough, one day I end up chasing a local shire councillor down the street, brandishing a monkey wrench, determined to brain the fat, pompous bastard.

My fault, of course, something he said that wasn't meant to sound the way it did. Anyway the shit hit the fan. What with me not willing to back down and several of the other big hats in the shire copping a fair share of Thommo's aggro. Suddenly the whole town's driving to Fisher's Bend twenty clicks up the road to fill up with petrol. BP gimme the bum's rush and a Thompson ain't running things mechanical no more in Currawong Creek.

So, being the brain-damaged fool I am, the next thing I try on is marriage. I'm lucky enough to still have my childhood sweetheart, Wendy McDonald, stick with me through all the flak. Her folk own Smoky Joe's Cafe, and, while I should have known better and she should have run a mile, we eventually get hitched.

I'm the luckiest bloke in the world but, of course, it doesn't take long for me to abuse the privilege. I come home pissed more often than not. I'm behind six months in the payments to the bank and they foreclose on me.

I'm now feeling ratshit all the time and getting these bad headaches which make me lose me temper soon as look at anyone. The rash, sweats and acne is getting worse, with no explanations for the reason. The chemist can't do nothing and the local quack shakes his head. I'm a flamin' mystery to the medical professional and if I wasn't such a big mean bastard, the quack at Veterans Affairs would probably accuse me of malingering so as to cop a disability pension.

Wendy and me are fighting. It's not only grog's the reason, I'm now into dope as well in an attempt to stay sane, or at least calm. Mixed with grog and pills it's not exactly acting like a health cure.

Then Wendy's old man drops dead in the middle of making a mixed grill for a tourist. Poor old bugger. Like me old man, he died on the job. But I've got to say this for him, in this one-horse town he played the music he wanted and he died to the strains of The Drifters. Wendy says he called the grease trap he's run since the fifties Smoky Joe's, because he never got over the songs of two Yanks, Leiber and Stoller, two Jewish blokes, Yanks, who, it seemed, loved Rock'n'Roll, Rhythm and Blues, and Jazz.

'Them two wrote songs that make people want to get up and dance. Not like the bloody rubbish you hear these days,' he'd snort to anyone he thought didn't dig the music that went all day and half the night in the cafe. He'd point to the jukebox which only had his records in it, he'd filled the coin slot with a drop of lead and fixed it so it played continuously without anyone tampering with it. If you didn't like the music at Smoky Joe's, tough titty, it was the only cafe in town. The Chink's was the only other place you could go to eat.

'You can't pay for music like that,' her old man would say, 'it's God's gift, Elvis, The Coasters, B. B. King and Miss Peggy Lee, now they knew how to sing a number. Mr Leiber and Stoller,' he'd say their names in a real respectful tone, 'may have been a couple of Jews but, I'm tellin' ya, music-wise they got it right every flamin' time.' It don't seem to matter to him that most people in Australia haven't like heard of some of these musicians. He has, and that's all that matters.

I reckon being took to your maker in the middle of a song you dig in a huge way is as good a way to die as a man can get. Like dying to your own background music.

Anyhow, we played Peggy Lee and Elvis at the funeral and, after the wake at Smoky Joe's, Wendy and me did the washing up and stacked the dead marines in the yard out back and just took up from where the old man left off.

We even kept all the old jukebox records and had them transferred to a continuous tape and played them in the same order her old man liked them played. Smoky Joe's is about as close to tradition as this piss-hole in the desert we call Currawong Creek will ever get.

Well, a man couldn't catch a fly with his mouth open, next thing Wendy's fallen pregnant. When she's well and truly up the duff, there's no money for help in the cafe and I'm as busy as a one-armed wallpaper hanger. I'm the short-order cook and serving at the tables, I'm chief bottle-washer and I'm standing behind the counter, scratching the rash on my crotch and try-ing to remember to smile at the locals. As well, I'm pushing Wendy's old girl around in her wheelchair, she's got what she calls her 'arty-ritus'.

The silly old cow spends most of every day chirping instructions at me like a cockatoo with a cuttlefish up its bum. She's also constantly reminding me that the 'Dearly Departed', which is how she has now come to address Wendy's old man Cec, left Smoky Joe's to her and Wendy, that half of the grease trap is hers. 'Tell me which half and I'll leave it for you to cook and clean and wash up, you stupid old cow!' I'd say, losing me block.

That gets her cackling on a treat, 'You don't deserve me daughter, you're no-good rubbish, not like your father or the Dearly Departed, salt of the earth them two!' For once in her life, she's right on the money. I couldn't get a kick in the balls in a street fight, I'm a bloody drongo. In between morning sickness Wendy's trying to make peace between us two and I'm not doing the right thing by her. So you can see we're not exactly playing happy families at Smoky Joe's Cafe.

The baby is born, it's a girl and I'm instantly in love and everything seems fine. Then when she's three she starts to slow down, lose energy, it doesn't take too long to know there's something wrong. We take her to the quack and then down to Sydney and she's diagnosed with leukaemia and has to have chemotherapy. If that don't work she'll need a bone-marrow transplant. The specialist in Sydney says she's got about a 20 per cent chance of making it. If the chemo doesn't kick in we've got to find a bone-marrow donor. The odds of finding one are enormous and it's gunna cost more money than I'm likely to make frying bacon 'n' eggs for the rest of me flamin' life.

'Could have happened to any family anywhere,' the fat quack at Repat says and shrugs his shoulders. 'It's not our responsibility anyway, the Veterans Entitlement Act does not include second-generation casualties, you'll have to take her to a public hospital. Next patient please, nurse!'

All I can think is Agent Orange. Agent Orange has done this to my kid, my beautiful little girl! It's my fault. It's Canberra's fault. It's them bastards in the Pentagon. We're stuffed. Wendy and me are stuffed for the duration. Nobody wants to know. Our precious little girl is just another statistic.

Then one morning early, while I'm hosing the pavement outside the Smoky Joe, a ute pulls up. 'Hey, Thommo!' a voice calls out. ''Ow ya goin', mate?'

It's Shorty di Maggio, same name as the baseball player who married Marilyn Monroe. He was our platoon sergeant and an army regular who had fought in the Malayan Emergency up 'til 1960, then stayed in the army afterwards. He was our sergeant in D Company of the 6th Battalion, The Royal Australian Regiment, 6 RAR. His job was to whip us into shape and get us combat-ready in Australia. I gotta hand it to the bastard, he did the job real good.

I remember the first time he stood in front of a

bunch of us blokes who'd just marched in from the school of infantry. He brought us all to attention. 'Platoon! Lissen in,' he says. 'This is your life from now on, you've joined the army and you will visit exotic and strange places like this shithole they call Vietnam and, when required, you will kill. That, gentlemen, is your mission.'

Shorty's folks own a farm about t'other side of Fisher's Bend in the irrigation area. Currawong Creek is in the Dry, we don't have irrigation. I haven't seen Shorty di Maggio since before Anna was born and here he is, same as ever.

Well, to cut a long story short, I fry him a plate of bacon 'n' eggs and throw in a bit of tomato, couple of snags, toast. He then proceeds to tell me he's been to see the two other blokes in the Riverina who came back from Vietnam and who were in our platoon and he's organising a reunion. He doesn't ask what I think of this idea, he's still the sergeant, which I guess when you've been in the regular army is a lifetime habit. You're not too interested in some grunt's opinion.

'How about we use Smoky Joe's Cafe for the big event? There's also seven of the blokes coming up from Sydney,' he says. 'Animal, Flow Murray, Bongface, Gazza, Killer Kowolski, Ocker Barrett and Macca.

Mate, it'll be like the movie, *The Dirty Dozen*. All of us back together!'

There are others in the platoon, of course. Of the original thirty men there are those who died in battle, some are 'Geographicals', which in our post-Vietnam lingo means they've gone bush or taken up a wandering lifestyle, and then there are some who've settled their lot, got their shit together or never lost it and don't want the renewed memories. So 'all of us' means Shorty's found some of the platoon who were at Long Tan and wants a reunion, though Christ knows why. I know better than to ask.

'Jesus, Thommo,' he grins, 'you're big and ugly enough to be a dead ringer for Lee Marvin.'

'Counting Spags and Lawsy from down the road that's only eleven of us,' I say. 'You can't have The Dirty Eleven, it don't work.'

'Yeah, well, you know what I mean, I couldn't locate the four others who were with us in the battle,' he says, impatient to continue. Fifteen of our platoon were Long Tan survivors so he's done pretty good.

'Fair enough,' I say.

Shorty's anxious to go on, jerking his thumb in the direction of the pub, 'Pub's practically next door where we can all stay the night, Spags and Lawsy, me too.

We'll be too pissed to drive home and the Sydney blokes will need late night and early mornin' drinking partners anyway. Can the pub take twelve?'

I don't remind him it's eleven. 'He can put us in army cots, keeps them out the back in the shed, three to a room, I'll book for ten, I can stay home.'

'Nah, twelve, you stay with us, we may end up with a stripper.'

I laugh, 'Not in this town, mate. The last stripper who come here turned out to be a poofter in drag.'

'Righto, but book for twelve anyway,' Shorty says, 'Never know your luck in the big city.'

I think about the glasses they gunna break and the mess I'm gunna have to clean up before Wendy gets home, but it's only a passing thought. I'm real pleased at the notion of the piss-up. It'll be good to see some of me Vietnam mates again, blokes who understand, who've been there.

'Besides, Thommo, you might as well make a buck out of the catering,' Shorty says. 'I'll bring the wine, it's me old man's own. We'll all throw in two bucks each for the food, another ten each for the other grog and a few bags of ice. The wine is irrigation plonk, but not too bad. We'll only have to drink it if we run out of beer after the pub's closed, bloody sight better than

21

most of the piss the local wogs make, even if I say so myself.'

I don't point out to him that he qualifies as a local wog as well. Shorty is built like a brick shithouse and is your born natural leader, and wog is not a term of endearment that suits him like it might most Eyetalians, Greeks or Lebbos. He used to say he joined the army to get away from his old man, who was trying to turn him back into an Eyetalian. He once told me, 'Me old man's a Sicilian and they only ever have one nationality and one home, some mud-cracked, crow-infested village up in the hills back of Bisacquino where they all end up killing each other and calling it tradition.' Besides, Shorty must be a throwback or something, because he's not your usual wog, he's got fair hair and blue eyes. He says it must have come about when the Greeks invaded Sicily about a thousand or so years ago. It seems that in those days the Greeks were blond with blue eyes like him.

I persuade Wendy to take Anna and spend the night with a girlfriend. I order in the grog, get in extra tucker, buns and mince for hamburgers and I bum a dozen wine glasses from Willy McGregor. He's dead chuffed at the overnight and agrees to leave a couple of cases of Flag Ale upstairs after the pub closes in case the boys get thirsty during the night.

Well, the night at Smoky Joe's is a big success or failure depending on how you look at it. It turns out most of us are in much the same boat since we got back. Can't settle down, hold a job, several of the guys are divorced. We're like a farmyard full of old chooks comparing our various ailments at the Country Hens Association Dinner.

Suddenly I realise I'm not alone, that my mates are going through the same hell as me. It's not just my imagination. Same headaches, rashes, panic attacks, nightmares, shit fights with wives, girlfriends or bosses, skin complaints, irrational behaviour, feeling half crook all the time. Some of my mates have been through the same tests and been told the usual bullshit about their psychological problems being their mothers' fault and that Agent Orange is harmless.

We're halfway pissed when Shorty calls us to attention by standing on his chair. 'Righto, lemme speak!' he shouts, tinging the lip of his wine glass with the blade of a knife. It's the same old Shorty di Maggio, platoon sergeant, always organising the mob. Reminding us, just by the way he stands, that he's permanent army and we're nashos. Though there was no difference in Vietnam, some of the nashos scrubbed up a damn sight better than the regulars and Shorty knows it.

Once when he was briefing us before going out on patrol he said, 'It's your flamin' duty to die for yer country and it's mine to see you don't.'

In Vietnam they said it was a corporal's war because in the jungle the corporal was the section leader, but I gotta tell ya, Shorty near ran the battalion and here he's at it again. Of all of us he seems the least affected or perhaps is best able to cope with civilian life. If he's had the rashes or acted irrational or suffers insomnia like the rest of us he don't say. Shorty always had his shit tightly packed together in an airtight plastic container, nothing seems to have changed. F'instance, we've all took to wearing our hair a bit long with sideburns down our cheeks and he's still got an army brushcut, short back 'n' sides, with his sideburns in line with the top of his ears.

'Thommo's in trouble!' he begins right off. 'No, not Thommo,' he corrects, 'Thommo's five-year-old kid, Thommo's little girl, Anna. She's got leukaemia and now has to have a bone-marrow transplant. First we've got to find a donor who's suitable and then we've got to find the bread for the operation!'

'Hey! Wait a minute,' I protest, 'I ain't said nothing to nobody about Anna, about our little girl!'

'Don't have to, mate!' Shorty says, his eyes sharp.

'We're not going to let your little girlie go down the gurgler because the gold braid in the Pentagon and all the President's men and their Canberra toadies won't take no responsibility! You know and they know it's AO what's done this to your little girl. Screw the FBI!'

'CIA,' I correct.

'Both,' he shoots back, 'we've got brothers in the States.'

'Yeah, well,' I mumble, feeling foolish, 'it's not your responsibility.'

'That's where you're dead wrong, mate,' Flow Murray chips in. 'Could've happened to any of us the same as it done to your kid! My little girlie was born with this nasty rash all over her body that won't go away.' He turns to the others, 'Yeah, man, let's do it for Thommo!'

Jesus, he's barely heard this weird proposal from Shorty and already he's all piss and wind. Flow gets his nickname because his surname is the same as the Murray River, the area where he comes from. That's in the first place, in the second he gets it because he'll always go with the flow. He doesn't have an opinion of his own. Someone says, 'Let's dip our heads in a bucket of piss so Charlie can't smell us?' and Flow goes looking for a bucket to piss in. He's what you'd call easily led, or maybe easygoing is a kinder way of putting it. But now he goes off like a string of crackers on Chinese New Year, what are we going to do? Sit back and cop the shit the Penta-fuckin'-gon's throwing at us or what?' he yells, fist in the air.

'Jesus, Flow, put a sock in it, will ya?' I say.

'Flow's right,' Shorty says, though he knows Flow's little ways as well as I do. Then several others also mumble their agreement. 'And what's more,' Shorty announces, 'I've got the plan of action!'

'Here we go,' Gazza says, rolling his eyes to the ceiling, 'Bloody sergeant's got a plan. Gawd help us!'

We all laugh.

'Whoa,' I say, 'not so bloody fast! Do you blokes know what kind of money it takes for a bone-marrow transplant?'

Shorty looks at me. 'Yeah, mate, I do. But it's not just you, Thommo. We're not just doing this for you and your kid.' He looks around, his gaze resting in turn on each of us. It's like the old days before the platoon went on patrol. He's getting us ready, leaching the fear out of us. 'We're gunna have to fight these miserable bastards, we'll start with Canberra and then we'll take on the Yanks if we have to!' He pauses, 'It's about justice, about givin' us a fair go.'

'Who, us? Fight them?' Macca protests, 'Come off it, mate, we're a bunch of no-hopers, the brain dead, Vietnam vets, the forgotten legion! Who are you kidding?'

Shorty turns around sharply. 'No one, mate, I'm not kidding. Matter of fact, I've never been more serious. There are blokes in America same as us, their vets are copping the same shit from the top brass in the Pentagon. We'll get in touch. Thommo's kid's going to die!'

'Hey, steady on, mate,' I say.

'Sorry, Thommo, but let's face the facts, mate. If she don't get a marrow transplant...' He doesn't finish and looks about the room. 'It won't just be her!' he says angrily, 'There are other kids too and some of us as well!' He shrugs his shoulders. 'Someone's got to do it, take responsibility, and we know it ain't gunna be those ingrates in Canberra or Washington!'

'Fight Canberra! Washington? It will take millions!' Ocker Barrett exclaims.

'So?'

'So where's the money going to come from?' Lawsy, who's a lawyer in Griffith, asks, 'You won the Opera House lottery or something?'

'We can get it, the money,' Shorty persists.

'How? Where?' several of us shout at the same time, my voice the loudest, I'm still annoyed at what he's said about my little girl.

Shorty puts up his hand to silence us, then waits 'til we're all concentrating on him. 'Dope. Marijuana!' he says, calm as all get-out.

We're all, you know, stunned. Dope, weed, selling it? Us? Shorty must 'ave gone troppo.

Then he continues, 'The nice clean little part-time hippies who marched in protest against us can't get enough of the stuff. It's the fashionable drug among the brave and the beautiful, the little boys and girls who think their protest marches won the war.'

'What about the dock workers who went on strike, useless bastards wouldn't load supplies to Vietnam?' Lawsy adds.

'Yeah, them too,' Shorty says impatiently, though I sense he's not too interested in including the dock workers, who've been screwing the nation around for generations anyway.

'There are two little valleys on the farm that's never been cultivated,' he continues. 'Mostly scrub and not too rocky, the soil's good, needs a bit of work and a drop of nitrate, that's all. It's hard to see from the air, nobody ever goes there, about seventy acres in all.'

Shorty looks around, 'Do you have any idea how much dope you can harvest on seventy acres irrigated?' he asks.

'Shit a brick!' says Spags Belgiovani, who's from another local Italian farming family just outside Griffith.

Shorty, it turns out, has taken over the family farm and his old man has gone back to Sicily to retire and be a proper Mafioso again. He's got enough dosh stashed away to last the distance and to make him the Consuleri or mayor of his mountain village and die properly from a blast of buckshot while he's eating pasta with chilli and cabanossi.

Basically, with the irrigation, the farm he's left his only son is rice, but the old man added a few vines and a couple of citrus orchards. What Shorty's inherited is a pretty good proposition, he sells his crop to the Rice Board at a guaranteed price, he's his own boss and he doesn't have to worry about a quid. What he's proposing, from his point of view, is pretty amazing. I mean, from where I sit, he's got everything to lose and I can't see he's got anything to gain.

'I've got someone I want you blokes to meet,' Shorty suddenly announces, 'Be back in a mo.'

Shorty hops down from his chair and leaves the cafe and we start to get into the piss and argue about the merits of his surprising proposition. After a few minutes I stand up and bring the room to silence by shouting louder than the rest of the mob. I'm a bit pissed but I know what I'm saying. 'Look, it's not on, fellas. What Shorty's proposed is serious.' I stop and look about me. 'We're not the men we used to be and we're not up against the provosts, the real cops will be onto us faster than you can wipe your arse one up, one down and one to polish. We have trouble enough keeping our own shit together, I for one, if the truth be known, couldn't get a fuck in a brothel. I don't want you blokes risking your freedom for me.' I pause, 'Wendy and me will manage somehow, but what Shorty's proposing, well, it's just not on, no way, Jose.'

'Bullshit!' Killer Kowolski shouts. He's ridden all the way from Sydney on his Harley and belongs to a bikie gang called 'Vets from Hell', which is painted on the back of his leather jacket. The gang is made up mostly of blokes who fought in Vietnam. 'We gunna do it, Thommo, bugger yiz!'

'Yeah, shit yes!' everyone shouts and then Bong-face jumps on the table. He's a skinny little runt but you wouldn't want to pick him or have a blue with him. Before he joined the regular army he fought in Jimmy Sharman's boxing troupe as a bantamweight, doing all the country shows. He's accustomed to going into the ring with big bastards off the land who are being egged on by their mates to have a go at the little Abo. He don't take no crap, no matter how big 'n' ugly his opponent is. Most Aborigines are more white-coloured than black these days, but Bongface looks like he's almost a pure blood and, I know, he's dead proud of the fact. When he smiles, his big white teeth take over his entire face and it makes you want to laugh, even if you're on patrol in the jungle quietly shitting yourself.

Most of his tribe are supposed to be able to track real good but Bongface grew up in Redfern and couldn't find an elephant's track in the snow. Maybe that's exaggerating a bit 'cause he's a bloody good scout, but he ain't exactly your didgeridoo-totin' tribesman. Abos weren't conscripted for Vietnam in the beginning, but like I said he'd volunteered and was a regular like Shorty. He has this sort of peripheral vision, something his kind is supposed to have and we don't. Like almost being able to see out the back of your head. He was the scout in our platoon and more than once he got us out of serious trouble, seen some movement in his flank we wouldn't have picked up, hit the deck and started firing. Being a scout is the shit job, you're the first to die if anything goes wrong. A mine, a booby trap, sniper, ambush, he is the first to cop the lot. Bongface would smile, 'I reckon the thing I'm most scared of is some dopey grunt from another battalion comin' across me in the jungle, blasting me off the flamin' planet thinking I'm a Nog.'

I'm a section leader, that's a corporal in the old army, and I gotta tell ya, I always felt a damn sight safer with the old Bongface up front having a gander before signalling us on.

His nickname come from this Chinese bong he bought from a Yank who got it in Hong Kong on R and R. It became like his signature. He don't drink so he took to dope. We'd cover for him when the provosts come snooping 'n' sniffin'. We'd be having a quiet grog or seven and he'd sit and pull contentedly on the mouthpiece of his bong. I remember how it had this red-enamel dragon decoration on the side and would be goin' *gurgle-gurgle* as he pulled the smoke through it and along the rubber tube. You could see him relaxing, getting the shit out of his system. Sometimes he'd giggle to himself like he knew something we didn't. Hence his name, 'Bongface Andrews'.

Well, he's on the table and he's holding a can of Coke up and says, 'I'm the only bloke here that's not pissed so I got the right to speak. Matter o' fact, I ain't even stoned.' We all shut up right off. It ain't like him to come forward, he's normally real quiet and don't say much at the best of times.

It's only now, with him holding the Coke, that I remember he'd never get on the piss. I mean he'd go along on a leave pass, but he'd drink Coke all night. Once, when I asked him why, he said, 'Yeah, well, blackfellas can't take the piss, Thommo, not like white-fellas, we ain't built right for it.'

'It's just beer, mate. Yank piss, Noggies Noggin, couldn't make a schoolgirl uncross her legs.'

'Nah, Thommo, that stuff don't work for us, it's what's destroying my people.' Which, when you think about it, is a pretty amazing admission to make on his part.

Now I look down at where he's been sitting and see he has brought a dozen cans of Coke along. I feel ashamed, I should've remembered, there's all the Coke he can drink and then some in the fridge. I should've told him to help himself, loaded him up for the dura-tion. He can have a smoke too. I've got some top weed, though he's probably got his own but is too shy to roll himself a joint now we've been parted a while. I can see he hasn't brought his bong along. Typical of the little bugger, probably thought the party might go on a bit and the local gendarmes could poke a face in and we'd all be compromised.

Funny that, hey, a bloke can get pissed as a newt, throw up on the pavement, go home and beat the shit out of his wife, so the neighbours have to call the cops. They turn up and put him to bed and persuade his missus not to lay charges, because basically he's a good bloke and is on the committee of the RSL. Then everybody goes home and the cops write it all down as just another Saturday night domestic. On the other hand, smoke a little weed quietly in a corner, minding your own business, and it's a drug arrest, a federal offence, you're in the slammer with the key thrown away. I'm buggered if I can see how that works. Shorty says it's because the government can't get any tax from dope smoking.

'Thommo, yiz full a shit,' Bongface begins real polite. 'Shorty's right, we gotta do something.' He brings on his big smile, 'Maybe we're no good at doing nothing much else, but we're all experts on covering our arses. We know how to look out for each other. Being aware like of the unexpected and knowing what to do when the shit hits the fan.'

'Dead right,' Flow offers again. 'Right on, mate.'

Bongface goes on. 'The government spent a lot of

bread training us and we learned it all in Vietnam. If we can't run somethin' like this we couldn't run a chook raffle in a pub full a drunks. Me personally, I've smoked every kind of weed you can name. I know where to get it, how to hide it, what's the going rate, how to talk to the customer.'

He shrugs his shoulders, 'Now all we've got to learn is how to grow it.' He turns to Spags Belgiovani, 'Spags here and Shorty know how to do that, so we've got no problem there neither.'

He gives us all his humungous smile, 'If it were anything else, I agree, we'd be history, but this thing we can do. We can do this like we done contact drill. Plan everythin' properly, react correctly in a crisis and take no chances.'

Killer Kowolski butts in, 'Shit yes, we can. We ain't gunna break down and 'fess up if a cop charges one of us with possession.'

I can't help meself and I think immediately of Flow, how he'd go with a big cop's hairy fist around his throat. But everyone cheers as Bongface steps down from the table and I keep this thought to myself. I'm beginning to get a funny feeling in me gut and I'm worried the whole thing is rapidly getting out of hand.

Then Shorty walks back into the cafe and he's got

this Nog in tow. Little bloke wearing a black suit and tie, like he works in a funeral parlour or something, white shirt, shiny shoes, snakeskin belt, hair lacquered down like a beetle's back and one ear missing. Shaved right off at the skull like it's been took for a trophy.

'Jesus, look what the cat brought in,' I hear Ocker whisper beside me.

'Holy shit!' It's Macca t'other side a me. Then we're all too gobsmacked to say anything more.

'Gentlemen,' Shorty announces, 'this is Nam Tran, he's a Vietnamese migrant and ex-Nog. Er, I mean, NVA Area Commander.' He grins, putting his hand on the man's shoulder like they're buddies. Standing like that, Shorty's nearly twice the width but no taller than this little Asian.

'Nam Tran here sort of slipped through the immigration when no one was looking,' Shorty adds. 'Him, and several of his mates and their families, live in Cabramatta, in Sydney. Now him and his mob also feel a tad aggro about Agent Orange, them being the unwilling victims thereof as well. Nam Tran here wants in. Wants to come on side. His people in Vietnam are still copping the shit from AO and all the herbicides we sprayed on them. Most of the Vietnamese migrants here are having trouble just like us.

Back home one in three births has a bad deformity. They've got kids in glass jars in the hospitals with two heads.' He looks around, fixing his eyes on each of us in turn. 'Whaddaya say, fellas?'

Well, there's a bit of discussion, associating with the enemy and so on and so forth, but we're all so completely took by surprise that soon enough everybody is nodding agreement. We all know Shorty doesn't do things impulsively, he must have done his homework and checked the little Noggie out. Now he grins, 'See, I told ya, Thommo, "The Dirty Dozen".' He looks around and says, 'There's a briefing tomorrow arvo, no more talk tonight. Tonight, gentlemen, we party . . . and if I may be permitted to say so, some of the brothers are missing, but it's bloody nice to see all yer ugly mugs again.'

'Christ, what am I going to tell Wendy,' I think to myself. She ain't gunna like this one little bit.

Chapter Two

As the night moved on a bit and we'd each had a beer or ten, the grog eventually got the better of us and we started to talk about the war. How it was.

Nam Tran's pulled up a chair and soon enough has a tinnie in his hand. He speaks pretty good English for a Noggie and we kind of forget he isn't one of us, that he's the one who'd been trying to kill us not that long ago.

Funny that, I don't know how it works, but it's like you've shared something no one else can understand, so when it's all over, you and the enemy, you're sort of, well, like brothers in arms?

Once the blokes reckoned they were with mates who knew what they were talking about, all the stuff you couldn't tell your family starts to come out. The point is, most vets find it bloody hard to make civilian friends, some never do. They develop what is known as the 'thousand-yard stare', looking into the distance with vacant eyes as though not wanting to engage. Which is true enough.

First the conversation goes mostly for laughs, the funny stuff, then later, when the grog has taken a hold, some of the other stuff that is not so funny, the shit, starts to come out.

'You know what really pisses me off?' Killer Kowolski starts off, 'The flamin' movies. People think Vietnam was like the Yank movies.'

'Hey yeah!' several of us shout, 'Right on!'

Me too, but I've got a theory. Remember we didn't actually fight with the Yanks and there is a reason why I reckon. They had a different kind of experience in Vietnam. We arrived trained as jungle fighters and they waged war with firepower, the more the better, and it seems it was the only way they knew how to fight. Shoot the crap out of everything, trees, mountains, buildings, tunnels, bridges, even rivers. I'm not saying they weren't brave. In some ways they were a lot braver than us, they'd go into a fight and stay with it when we would withdraw from enemy contact, prepared to wait for better odds.

Maybe it was the right way to fight in Eastern

Europe, Russia and East Germany and places like that. But it was a shit of a way to fight in Vietnam, where you seldom came face to face with an enemy that would stand up and fight you front on, weapon for weapon, and so on. So, maybe their movies show some of that experience, the chaos and the firepower, not the long, hard slog in the deep j, hunting Noggie, which was our experience.

I've given up trying to tell people to take no notice of the Yank movies when they're talking about us. The problem with Vietnam was that it was a different kind of war, one that people wanted to forget. Then they learned this new Hollywood version all over again from going to *The Deer Hunter*, *Apocalypse Now* and a bunch of other movies that nudged the truth aside for the sake of the box office.

Lawsy, who's about the smartest of us all, though maybe Shorty is up there with him, says, 'Yeah, you know, scene one, open on a lot of spaced-out guys who come swooping down in choppers in a hot insertion to kill old men, women and children and waste their village, rock music blasting to the heavens. Then, on the way home, blow up an entire mountain and quickly dissolve to an underground shot as the contained therein start to collapse, Nogs inside dying in their hundreds.

Then, if the movie director happens to remember, you might get an occasional scene in the next two hours when Charlie gets into a personal fight with the grunts on the ground, one of which always turns out to be a beautiful and defiant Nog chick, but not before the Ho Chi Minh trail has been completely eliminated.' He gives a short laugh, 'Beats the crap out of the truth.'

'Or, the other way around,' Gazza interrupts, 'The women and kids kill the American warriors, who also occasionally die in a genuine ambush by Charlie.'

This brings another laugh because it's right on the money. Everyone agrees, what's been shown on the movies is about 95 per cent pure bullshit. My theory is took no notice of, though I still reckon I'm halfway right.

'Talk about birds,' Spags now chips in, 'I'm with this real good sort, a bit classy for me maybe, but I reckon I'm doing okay. I've bought her a couple of drinks, brandy alexanders, a few more of them and, no risk, she'll be feeling no pain, the hem on her mini is creeping up near the promised land and I can see the V of her underpants.'

'Knickers,' Gazza says, 'They's knickers, mate.'

'Not knickers! Jesus, that's what yer mum wears,' Flow, already half cut, says, 'They's panties, where you been all yer life?'

'Lingerie,' Lawsy says, 'You said she was a classy bird.'

'Leave off, will ya? Who's telling this story?' Spags protests. 'I can see her pants, they're red and made of shiny stuff and I'm in heaven. Could be the night. Buy her a bit of supper, bottle of good plonk. Never know what could happen in the big city.

'Then some silly bastard in the pub shouts out, "You were in Vietnam, weren't you, Spags?" He's havin' an argument with his mates.

'"Yeah," I say, though I'm not real happy to be interrupted.

'"Did you blokes use Yank rifles?" he yells over at me.

'"SLRs and the Owen guns were made in Australia and the M16s were bought from the Yanks," I tell him and turn back to this bird, so he'll know I'm not that keen to be yesterday's bloody hero.

'She looks at me, pulls back on her stool and her neck jerks back like she's just copped a straight left on the chin. "You were in Vietnam?" she asks, "Vietnam?" but she don't wait for the answer. "You fought in Vietnam!" she says a third time, her baby blues stretched to the limit.

'"Yeah," I say.

'Jesus H. Christ! You should a seen her expression. Suddenly she's gone off a me like a bucket of prawns left in the sun.

'"What about My Lai and that Lieutenant Calley?" she says. "You killed women and children! Little kids! Old women! Napalm!" She's poking her finger into me chest.

'"Hey, wait on, that's bullshit! We done no such thing! The Yanks done that one."

'She's snarling at me now and she's up off her seat and wiggles her bum so her mini comes down an inch or two and she's tugging at it like she's trying to cover her knees as she backs off.

'"Yes, you did, you bastard!" she snaps, then walks out the pub. I follow her, protesting, flappin' me arms and shrugging me shoulders just like my old man. Blokes in the pub are turnin' and looking at me, laughing, thinking I'm having a blue with me bird.

'I get outside on the pavement and put my hand on her shoulder, "Wait on, Angela, you're wrong, I ain't ashamed of nothing I done in Vietnam!"

'She shakes my hand loose, then she does her block, "Piss off, you miserable bastard," she says and walks away, leaving me standing there like a shag on a rock. All I can see is her beautiful arse as she clip-clops down

43

the pavement in her high heels. I just blew ten bucks and I ain't done nothing she's said I done. Fuck, what was that about? I says to meself.'

We laugh, but it's not at Spags. We've all been through something like he's just told. That certain look when you tell them you're a Vietnam vet, one eyebrow slightly raised, chin forward, head to one side, then eyes looking downwards when you try to explain.

I don't know of any atrocities we committed. We didn't waste villages to get a hard-on. I don't know anyone who fought with me in Vietnam who knew of any incidents we ought to be ashamed of. Maybe they did things to captured prisoners at Nui Dat, but, if they did, I never heard about it.

I do know Charlie had a few nice little habits he'd use on his own kind as well as on us. He'd bury village people alive if they didn't pay their rice tax. He'd kill and torture when he thought information was being withheld.

We saw the results so I know that much was true. You could never truly relax, they were always at it, acid in a bottle of Coke, snake venom injected into a mango, slivers of glass in ice cubes served in a drink, even bombs hidden on a baby's body as a booby trap.

Fair enough, I suppose. If our country was being

invaded I expect we'd do the same. I heard of one time when the Yanks had gone into a village and inoculated the kids against smallpox and that night the Viet Cong came and chopped off the arms of every kid above the inoculation mark as a lesson to the villagers not to fraternise with the enemy.

I didn't see that, I admit, so it may be propaganda put out by our side. There were more rumours around than there were Vung Tau prostitutes and that's rumour saturation. If you didn't actually see something with your own eyes in Vietnam or hear it fair dinkum from one of your mates, you took no notice. If you heard it on the American Forces Radio, that was 100 per cent pure bullshit. But, as I said, atrocities are a part of war and practised by both sides and, far too often, the victims are women and kids. Vietnam was no different.

Shorty starts talking now, doing what he's always done, explaining things. I remember now that he thinks of himself as a bit of a war historian, him being all those years in the permanent army like.

'The problem begins with the war we were in,' he says. 'It turned out different to the other wars Australia's been in. We marched away heroes and come back to a country that didn't want to know us. It's going out, drums and bugles, flags flying, sheilas crying, then, four years later, they flew our wounded back at two in the morning when the whole bloody country's asleep. That's never happened before to a soldier fighting for Australia.'

Ocker Barrett interrupts, grinning. 'I had to bang on the kitchen door for twenty minutes to wake my mum up. I'm doing it with me elbows because of me bandaged hands and it's hurting like hell. When she opens the door, she's got her curlers in, them twisted bits of paper, and she's got the same crook-looking dressing-gown she wore before I left for Vietnam. She thinks she's seen an apparition or something, me standing there at the kitchen door at four o'clock in the morning with me hands bandaged!

'"Is that you, David?" she says, real frightened, stretching out her hand to touch me, see it's really me and not a ghost with white bits sticking out the sleeves.'

'Me too!' Bongface laughs. 'Exact same! Me old man come out to answer the door, coughin' and swearin', he's still half pissed from the night before, "Who the fuck are you?" he asks me, then begins to shout for me mum. "Mary, Mary, our boy's dead, they's gorn an' killed him!"' Bongface laughs. 'He thinks I'm come out of the Dreamtime to visit him or somethin'!'

The rest of us came back on the HMAS *Sydney*, which was known as the 'Vung Tau Ferry'. We marched in Sydney but the crowds, that's a laugh, the people who bothered to come out, didn't exactly give us a ticker-tape parade! I have to be honest, I didn't give a continental, I was home again and Wendy come down from Currawong Creek and was there to meet me. Me mum's been long passed away and the old bloke died while I was away, so Wendy's the nearest thing I have for a relative.

Shorty carries on with his lecture to us, we've heard it all before, but we let him rave on a bit anyway, don't do no harm being reminded. 'Like I said before, Vietnam was different. To cut a long story short, some silly bugger in America comes up with something called The Domino Theory.' Shorty looks around, making sure we're all still paying attention.

'You know, like dominoes set up on their end in a long line, tap the first one, it hits the next, knocks it over and so on until they've all fallen down.

'Some prize prick in the Pentagon persuaded the world that Vietnam was the number-one communist domino controlled by China and if we didn't take it out of the line, teach them once and for all not to try anything on, then Laos, Cambodia, Thailand and so on and so forth would follow until they overran Australia.

47

'Every bastard buys it, in particular the Catholic Church who are very big in Vietnam, they put the heavy on the DLP, who go to work on the Liberals and Bob Menzies. Pronto, we're in boots 'n' all.

'Sounds bloody stupid now, but at the time with the big Russian bear grunting and thumping its chest and the mighty Chinese dragon huffin' and puffin', the idea of them two big Commie countries threatening our way of life sounded pretty bloody convincing to us local cowboys who thought we were bulletproof anyway. We had to stop the number-one domino falling and we were just the blokes to do the job.'

Shorty senses he's goin' on a bit. 'Okay, there's not much more,' he says. 'We were going to send in the cavalry and come home heroes, the new ANZACS. The folk across the pond, our good neighbours the Kiwis, were comin' along as well, only a handful, a token artillery battery to start with and an infantry rifle company later on but that made us sort of ANZACS. History repeatin' itself, Gallipoli and all that.'

We all clap, sending him up. 'Jesus, Shorty, you ain't changed none, still got the gift of the gab. You would've made a bloody good DJ bullshitting on American Forces Radio, mate,' Lawsy says to our laughter.

Yeah, but Shorty is damn right. We reckoned we'd

done a good job and deserved the same as the diggers in the other wars.

I've never marched in an Anzac Day Parade, haven't joined the RSL neither. Some of the blokes tried to do both and soon got jack of being told by some half-pissed old digger that they hadn't been in a real war, not like the Second World War, that we were a bunch of little boys who liked to whinge. Maybe they didn't understand the different nature of the Vietnam guerilla war, but when the RSL sided with the government over the Agent Orange issue, that was the finish. We didn't want a bar of them or the parade.

Shorty's not quite finished yet, despite the applause that tells him we know the rest. He looks at Gazza and Bongface. 'Yeah, you're dead right. They were telling us that what we done and what we'd been through meant bugger all. "Go home, little fella, have a good night's sleep and forget you ever went to Vietnam and fought with our good friends, the Yanks. Mind you, they're still our good friends, 'All the way with LBJ' but just don't talk about it. Okay? Now bugger off, soldier."

'I know we weren't alone in this. The big brush-off. The brothers in America copped the same treatment as us and they're suffering from all the same problems

Vietnam caused. They've got the same kind of shit-for-brains leaders. What pisses me off is the politicians who started it all and then ran for cover and Veterans Affairs and the RSL who treated us like we'd disgraced the colours, that we'd let the fighting tradition of Australia down.'

'Yeah, remember when some bastard reporter writes in the *Sydney Morning Herald*,' Ocker now says, 'how we were issued with American rations and served hot three-course meals delivered by chopper when we were out on patrol? Gordon flamin' Blow, or whatever that Frog who does French cooking is called. Turkey and jello, canned fruit, chocolate, cookies and Coke. How we was livin' in the lap of luxury, about the soft war for dolly birds that we're fighting in! I'd like to have found that bastard and taken him and his typewriter into the jungle for a couple of weeks! Make the bloody idjit eat his words!'

'Jesus, yes! Them Yank ration packs,' Animal shouts, missing the whole point, 'They was bloody good!'

Animal was the only one who would carry the Yank rations intact, the rest of us would get rid of at least half the stuff in them. They weighed a bloody ton, about three times as much as our own rations. One Yank ration meal was more than our own rations for the entire day. When you went out on patrol your pack and gear weighed 80 pounds, we'd even cut off the handle of our toothbrushes, squeeze half the toothpaste out the tube, anything to keep the weight down. You carried nothing you didn't have to, in the heat it was much better to eat less than carry more.

Animal's got his name because he'll eat and drink anything and throw up and start all over again and, as well, make a serious attempt to screw every bar girl in Vietnam.

Here's an Animal joke he tells everyone he meets: 'Vietnam is a place where a Nog in black pyjamas carries two buckets of shit across his shoulders using one stick and then uses two sticks to eat a bowl of shit.' See what I mean?

Macca now comes in. 'Christ, yes, I remember I once got one o' them Chinese fortune cookies in my Yank rations and I break it open and feed the crumbs to the chomper ants and read me fortune on this slip of paper inside. "Your ship of life will always sail in calm, contented waters, romance will come your way by the next full moon." We're in the second day of a three-week operation in the jungle, it's full moon in two nights and just after sunset on the night of the full moon, we walk into a group of Viet Cong strolling along the river and I reckon I've got a choice; I can fuck Charlie and find true romance under the light of the moon or sink the ship of contentment and shoot the bastard who's shooting at me and get some real satisfaction.'

Rations, yes, it's true, we sometimes used American rations and they were better than our own, which wouldn't have been too hard. But here's the first thing most people don't understand about us and the Americans. Though we fought in the same war, we didn't fight in the same areas. We had our own area of operation to fight in, us in Phuoc Tuy province and them pretty much everywhere else in South Vietnam.

We didn't even get invited to any of their concerts when Bob Hope and all of their sexy singers and movie stars came to entertain. As a matter of fact, our company didn't even see Col Joye and Little Pattie when they come to entertain us, because we was otherwise occupied in a stoush down the road that's come to be called the Battle of Long Tan.

True, we were supported by American air power and their choppers, along with our own. They often brought out our wounded or ferried us from the Kanga Pad at Nui Dat to our operational areas or directly into combat. This last was known as a 'hot insertion'. They also dropped ammunition where we needed it, and their assault helicopters, called Cobras, rocketed and strafed in really close support for us.

I recall one time, it was early morning and we were out on patrol, when suddenly the sky lit up as a squadron of B52 bombers dumped several hundred 750-pound bombs on the Long Hai Hills just ahead of us. The earth shook, like there was an earthquake going on. Some of us were thrown to the ground.

We'd been using our hexe stoves at the time to 'brew up' and I can remember the stove and the mugs on them just took off and these arcs of boiling water criss-crossing like in slow motion twenty feet above the ground. We were thrown onto our arses, yet the bomb drop was several miles away. It was the most awesome spectacle I've ever seen. If Charlie was somewhere underneath copping this load of instant death out of a drizzling monsoon sky, and I guess they must have been, the Long Hai Hills were a favourite place for the Noggies to build bunkers and underground caves, they would've been bloody uncomfortable for a bit. I'll say this for the Yanks, they never did things by halves.

We also used their artillery a lot of the time. Matter of fact, located about a mile from Nui Dat was an

American battery of self-propelled eight-inch guns, really big buggers. They'd be used for long-range targets or for targets that needed busting open. You could always hear their big *kerboom* over the sound of the other artillery. You could usually sleep through a salvo of the other guns but not those big bastards. And sometimes they'd fire H & I all through the bloody night. H & I means 'Harassment and Interdiction'. Our artillery would fire at irregular intervals at VC resupply routes and known areas thick with Charlie's bunker systems. The idea was to keep the VC from thinking they owned the night, which they most surely did. Make them know that something nasty could land in their midst at any time and almost anywhere.

I suppose it worked, nobody really knew.

'Remember H & I?' I now say, 'The big guns goin' all day, all night. Remember how every time one of the real big bastards went off it would make the dunny seats in the camp fly open? If you happened to be sitting on one having a quiet crap, you got a blast of hot air up the arse that fair made you take off.'

This brings another laugh. Funny how you remember the little things. At Nui Dat they'd dig a big pit about fifteen yards long and put a cement slab over it with holes to accommodate about thirty cement cones upon which they placed dunny seats, the whole thing in the open, no walls, just a tin roof to keep out the sun and then the rain in the monsoon season.

Naturally, after a while, the pit would get a trifle on the nose and besides would become the home to all manner of insects who were partial to a bit of a chomp on the family jewels.

'Remember The Blowfly?' I ask and there's nods all round. The Blowfly was a private in the Hygiene Unit. He'd mix three gallons of diesel fuel with maybe a quarter of petrol and pour it down the dunny holes and set the whole box and dice alight, kill the creepy crawlies and turn the turds to ash in one big *whoof* of flame.

One day something happens to The Blowfly, he's reported sick or he's got a leave pass or something and they send in an assistant Blowfly. The new bloke gets the mix vicki-verka and a quarter of a gallon of diesel with three of petrol and blows the whole lot to kingdom bloody come. We reckon there must have been VC in the jungle wearing dunny seats for collars, wondering what next the Yanks at H & I were gunna think of doing to them.

The only thing the movies seemed to get half right is showing the street scenes in Saigon City and other towns, the whorehouses, the girls and the cheap bars with the walls made out of flattened beer cans. The strip. You could see the same thing in Bangkok or pretty well in any other place in Asia.

In Vung Tau, where we'd go for a seventy-two-hour break, this particular area was known as the front beach and the back beach, with 'The Flags' the centre of the front beach. There were hundreds of bars and brothels, or brothels with bars as most of them were. The front beach was where we went and the back beach was out of bounds. The rumour was the back beach was where the Viet Cong went for their rest and recreation.

The subject of Vung Tau now comes up and Flow pipes in, 'There was this time Animal and me got separated from you blokes at The Flags. We're a bit pissed and Animal's thrown up a couple of times and someone's told him the Viet Cong pussy is better than our own, that they're keeping the best for the enemy. I'm the only one who's stupid enough to believe this or to think it's a good idea. So him and me decide to go to the back beach.

'We get to this bar and it's filled with Vietnamese blokes dressed the same as usual in black pyjamas. We order a couple a beers and two bar girls come and sit with us. They don't look much different to the ones we've just left behind. Pretty soon the locals are sending us over half a dozen beers and we're returning the favour and we're having a bit of a laugh, though we can't understand their lingo nor they ours. Then suddenly one of them says something and they all get up and go out the back and next thing they're back and they're carrying AK47s.

'"Shit, Flow!" Animal whispers, "It's time for the last rites and there's no flamin' priest in sight!" But the Viet Cong smile and nod and give us the thumbs up as they leave. Animal turns to me and says, "Whaddaya say, Flow? I think I prefer the sheilas back at The Flags!"'

'Yeah, and I got the clap that time too!' Animal remarks.

This brings up a real big snort all round, because Animal got the clap every time. In fact about 25 per cent of the battalion had it at one time and the MO decides it's way out of order and he calls each company separately into the mess for a bit of a chinwag and general dressing-down. 'You've all been issued with condoms and you're not using them!' he shouts down the microphone. 'The VD statistics in the battalion have reached alarming proportions and you've got to clean up your act!'

The doc walks up to this big blackboard and he takes a piece of yellow chalk and on one side he writes a huge '60%', filling half the blackboard, and on the other side he writes '20%' just as big.

'Right, get this into your thick skulls, gentlemen,' he says. 'Sixty per cent of the prostitutes in Vung Tau have venereal disease and 20 per cent have tuberculosis!' He pauses to let this sink in.

Suddenly Animal shouts from the back, 'Does that mean we only fuck the ones who cough?'

For us, though, Vietnam wasn't an occasional leave pass to the bright lights of Vung Tau but endless patrols and operations in the jungle, keeping Charlie on the move. Sometimes these operations would last five weeks where you seldom got to wash and you shaved every morning using the sweat on your face for lubrication. At night, if you were lucky, you erected your hutchie. Often, though, we just wrapped the hutchie around us and threw ourselves on the ground to sleep.

You suffered prickly heat, crotch rash and footrot. The dust in the dry season was filled with fleas and when the monsoon rains came they brought the leeches and the mozzies and the mud. You'd spend an hour every night under your hutchie, wet and miserable, burning the leeches off every part of your body with the tip of a cigarette.

That was just for openers and had nothing to do with the fact that Charlie was stalking you and you him. If you were an ordinary infantryman, a grunt, you knew nothing about the operation you were on and told bugger all. Fortunately, in our platoon we had Shorty. He had the ear of the platoon commander and, if the truth be known, probably the company commander as well. Most of the time he seemed to have some idea of what we were supposed to be doing and where we were supposed to end up and he'd tell us corporals who ran the platoons, so that, as section leaders, we'd know what was expected of us. But the grunts in many of the other platoons didn't know if they were comin' or goin'.

We were the best-trained jungle fighters in Vietnam. Possibly the world. Our instructors at Canungra in Queensland had fought in Korea and in the Malayan Emergency and some had even fought in Vietnam with the training team. They knew what to expect, how to train us in the craft of jungle fighting for what they knew was to come.

But, for your average grunt, it was still a bloody big mystery. We were against blokes in black pyjamas with

AK47s who were fighting and dying for their country, their wives and kids, and maybe even for something else they believed in. We were chasing them around their own jungle backyard shitting ourselves. And what for? Buggered if we knew. There was a saying: 'If I had a farm in Vietnam and a home in hell, I'd sell the farm and go home.'

As the evening wore on and we got really pissed the blokes started to talk about the hard parts. I suggest some tucker before I get too pissed to make it. I've got meat pies in the oven but I warn them they're best left unet, I explain that Willy McGregor makes them up the pub from scrag-ends. 'They're for the drunks.' I'm about to go on and say we only sell them from the cafe to the boongs when I remember Bongface. 'They're rat-shit,' I say instead.

'I'll have a couple of them dog's eyes,' Animal calls out. I can see he's fair dinkum. 'Never tasted a meat pie I didn't like with a drop of dead horse.'

I start to put together a couple of dozen hamburgers and fry chips for the mob. I want them to be good and you can't make a good burger 'n' chips if you're pissed and, besides, I'm not the world's best short-order cook, but a bloke's got his pride.

So I'm behind the counter making burgers and as

each bloke talks there's increasingly long silences. I can't remember what was said exact, not like I do the funny stuff, the humour. Now the brothers are slurring their speech a bit, digging down where they haven't been for a while, searching for words that don't come easy or don't come at all. There are no correct ones, there are never gunna be the right words to kill the pain. We're all feeling it. Sometimes what they don't say is the worst pain of all.

But it makes no difference, I was there with them and in between the sizzle of the onions on the hotplate, the deep fry and the feel of the raw mince in my hands, I can smell the fear returning. It's always with you, just below the surface, always will be. Mostly the talk is stuff about the jungle, goin' in scared and comin' out a month later with a few more live sunrises and sunsets to your credit. Nobody talks about Long Tan.

It's hard to describe coming out of the jungle, out of combat, getting back behind the wire. You've made it one more time, but there was always a next time, the hole in your guts never gets filled, the fear never stops. When you've been out on patrol for maybe ten days or three weeks or more you never seem to come out of it.

Every step you make every day, right down to finding a place to have a crap. Wiping your arse real slow so the movement won't disturb the foliage, give your position away. In the field we were issued with three pieces of shit paper per day, one up, one down and one to polish. When you got back to the safety of Nui Dat with all the crap paper in the world, you find yourself breaking off just three pieces, the habit, the fear, still with you even when you're polishing your arsehole in safety.

I've just said how it was coming out of the deep j. But what I'm talking about is the anticipation. The days of nothing happening but knowing something could any moment. Know what I mean? In fact, while in the boonies it was almost a relief to be up against some real combat. Charlie firing at you, sending over his mortars, returning fire, havin' a go, working out his range. That was tolerable, you could take that. Warriors havin' a go at each other.

It was the silent war that broke you down. Every step of every day, watching Bongface ahead, expecting him to be blown to kingdom come every next step he took, or have him spring a booby trap or dive for cover and yell, 'Contact Front!' Then behind him the machine gun moves forward to the higher ground or to the right and opens fire in support of the scout. Now you're in action, your rifle group moves around you and, as section commander, you can give them orders, maybe a quick flank attack on the enemy. All this is expected, you've been trained for it, you're a warrior doing your job, best you can.

Then out you'd come, your patrol or operation over. If you were unlucky, minus a couple of your mates wrapped in their hutchies sent ahead. The worst was seeing your flying dead leave you in the jungle as the dustoff came in and carted them off above the treetops to the morgue, and you having to stay behind. Sounds weird, don't it? Thinking the dead are better off than you. Or some bloke still alive, holding his guts in his hands, seen as a lucky bastard. Shit, shit, shit.

The last thing I saw of my mate Mo were the soles of his boots sticking out from his waterproof hutchie, which I'd used to cover him. A single yellow bamboo leaf, shaped like the head of a Zulu spear, was stuck to the heel of his left boot. I rushed forward as the dustoff lifted him up from the ground, the chopper blades above my head a wind-rush of cool air in the humidity, and grabbed the leaf off of his heel and shoved it into the pocket of my greens.

I've still got it, stuck onto a picture of him and me in a whorehouse in Vung Tau. We're holding a bottle of beer up to the camera with two pretty little whores. Wendy says they look like porcelain dolls. They're sitting on our laps, we were both big bastards, and the girls look like schoolkids. Probably should have been at another time and in a better world than this one.

You'd come off patrol or some operation and have your first real wash for five weeks. There was always the moment when you took off your greens, which stank of sweat and mud and dirty humans. You'd shower, hoping that by some miracle the hot water would clean not only the outside but what was dirty on the inside as well.

You'd get into civvies and if you were real lucky be granted a seventy-two-hour leave pass to Vung Tau. You'd be so pumped up you'd laugh at anything, any small prank played on a mate no matter how stupid, and then you'd get drunk and have sex and get drunk and have sex and get drunk and have sex until it all became a blur, a bottle of Ba Mui Ba beer down one hole and your cock in another. Drinking piss and fucking, the combat soldier's eternal antidote to stop the fear in his gut and kill the poison in his soul.

Then back to Nui Dat with the tension still in your entrails. The terror still there, knowing you'd soon be out in the jungle again with the Noggies finding a hundred ways to kill you, the weird *crackle-pop* of their AK47s burned into your memory forever.

We didn't wear underpants in the jungle because they chafed and made the prickly heat rash in your crotch worse. But when we put on civvies we'd put on undergear as well. Then when you returned and it was time to go into the jungle again, you'd give away the Y-fronts. That was it, the real deep fear of dying returned when you put on your fresh greens and let your balls dangle free.

In less than an hour your greens would be soaked through from the humidity you could never escape. The first of the razor-sharp grass seeds had worked through your trousers and you knew there'd be a hundred more and you'd have to wait 'til nightfall to pluck the bastards out. Your pack bit into your shoulders and rubbed them raw and your webbing belt pushed down on the bones of your hips with the weight of water bottles, a dozen magazines, grenades and all the other soldiering crap you carried in the pouches hanging off it, not to count yer crossover ammo belt. You weren't in the jungle ten minutes and you knew it was gunna be a bloody long day, and the fear was back and the fear was you.

Righto then, let's begin at the beginning. And the beginning is a brown envelope in the post box to tell you the good news that your number just come up and you are one of the chosen ones. So here's the next mis-conception. We didn't whinge and tell ourselves, 'Why me? Why not some other joker?' Most of us were stoked. We were going to war like our fathers and our grandfathers, we were going to be warriors, the lucky bastards, true to the flag.

On the day I reported at the recruitment centre there were a bunch a protesters with banners outside, well, not exactly a bunch, four women, fat and ugly. Their banner said, 'Say "No!" to Vietnam! Save our Sons!' They were chanting, 'Don't spill our blood in Vietnam!' over and over. One of the fat sheilas was shouting and wagging her finger at me and I remember thinking, 'You stupid old cow, you've probably never had a good root in your life!' Twenty-year-old warriors-to-be don't want to be saved, they know they're personally bullet-proof anyway and this stupid bitch was trying to stop me having my own war adventure.

I reckon the people thought it was the right thing to do, to support our American mates. Blokes bought you a beer in the pub. 'You're doin' your bit, son,' some of the old-timers would say, 'Good on ya, mate.'

There was some stuff in the papers about how we shouldn't be going, but public opinion or, anyway, the stuff I heard on the box and goin' on around me and on the radio, like, was pretty encouraging.

We were sent to Kapooka near Wagga Wagga in central New South Wales, that was July 1965, I think. Kapooka was okay, a lot of shouting and drill, rifle practice, fitness, lectures, route marches, inspection, latrine duty and whatever else the RDI (Regimental Duties Instructor), a regular army platoon sergeant, thought would successfully beat the crap out of us.

Kapooka was all the usual bullshit the army carries on to turn a raw recruit into a totally responsive, rigidly starched uniform with boot caps endlessly polished and brought to mirror gloss. There used to be a joke, you polished your boot caps 'til you could see your face in them, that's so when you were standing close to a bird you could look down into your boot caps and see up her skirt.

I don't remember all that much about it to tell you the truth, I was too bloody tired most of the time, but a good few recruits got sent home because they didn't cut the mustard.

There's a poem written by a bloke named Bruce Dawe that sums up the instructors at Kapooka to a T. I've learned it off by heart and I hope he don't mind me using it now.

Weapons Training

And when I say eyes right I want to hear
those eyeballs click and the gentle pitter-patter
of falling dandruff   you there what's the matter
why are you looking at me   are you a queer?
look to your front   if you had one more brain
it'd be lonely   what are you laughing at
you in the back row with the unsightly fat
between your elephant ears   open that drain
you call a mind and listen   remember first
the cockpit drill when you go down   be sure
the old crown-jewels are safely tucked away
   what could be more
distressing than to hold off with a burst
from your trusty weapon a mob of the little yellows
only to find back home because of your position
your chances of turning the key in the ignition
considerably reduced?   allright now suppose
for the sake of argument you've got
a number-one blockage and a brand-new pack
of Charlies are coming at you
   you can smell their rotten
     fish-sauce breath hot on the back
of your stupid neck allright now what

are you going to do about it?   that's right grab and check
the magazine man it's not a woman's tit
worse luck or you'd be set   too late you nit
they're on you and your tripes are round your neck
you've copped the bloody lot just like I said
and you know what you are?   you're dead dead dead

Then it was on to the School of Infantrymen at Ingleburn, near Sydney. There we learned our contact drills,
section attacks, platoon attacks, patrolling, digging
weapon pits, firing M60s, Owen guns and throwing
grenades, and so on until we dropped with exhaustion.

I know we thought we were pretty ridgy-didge when
we come out of Ingleburn. We could march in a straight
line, fire a rifle, stop on command with a single sound as
our boots hit the deck. We'd lost most of our puppy fat
and we could run a mile with a full pack and rifle and we
could do all the things a warrior has to know to stay
alive. Ha bloody ha, if only we'd known what lay ahead!

A mob of us were sent to join 6 RAR at Enoggera
Barracks in Queensland. That was when Shorty got
hold of us. Christ! He made our training at the School
of Infantrymen seem like a sheila's knitting class. We
ran miles with full gear, we practised mounting and
dismounting drills for armoured personnel carriers and

jumping on and off bloody choppers 'til our legs went to jelly. We practised ambushes, we dug holes, built barbed-wire obstacles, practised clearing mines and booby traps, we fired our weapons and endlessly practised patrolling. We worked sixteen hours a day in the bush and sometimes Shorty kept us going for days without sleep.

We thought that what Shorty was putting us through was tough, but really it was just a warm-up for Canungra, the jungle training centre in south-east Queensland. They must have searched the whole flamin' country to find this particular shithole. That's what it was, a big hole with hills called yamas surrounding it, filled with muddy water that might as well have been shit. It felt like shit. Tasted like shit and smelled like shit when you fell into it. And it stuck to you like shit sticks to a blanket.

We'd go out on patrol among the yamas, where they'd set up all sorts of so-called nasty surprises, shooting galleries and sneaker ranges. With the shooting galleries, cut-out targets would suddenly appear which we were supposed to destroy with a single shot, Audie Murphy style. Most of them looked as though they'd been there forever with no bullet holes to show, which gives you some idea of how effective we were gunna be in the killing fields of Vietnam.

The sneaker ranges I have to say were a bit more predictable. We'd be sneaking along a path, SLR at the ready, and the instructor would pull at some concealed rope or wire and, lo and behold, a target would be facing us. We were required to put three shots into it in the time it took us to blink. After a while, we could do this. I hasten to say, not because we were any better than before with the shooting galleries but because the bushes and foliage in the area of the target were so shredded by blokes who'd been before us that we could anticipate the enemy before the wire was released and so had plenty of time to get the three shots away.

Later, in Vietnam, when the same thing happened for real and this VC suddenly appeared in front of me, I seem to remember shitting my greens. No, I mean it, I shat meself. Fortunately I think he did too. I finally got the first three rounds off, all of which missed and the VC scarpered into the jungle before I could get another crack at him. So, Canungra style, I destroyed all the surrounding shrubbery in the direction he'd taken.

We never found him, not even a blood spot. I guess I missed Charlie with about a hundred rounds fired into a bamboo thicket and, I remember, I had a hard time convincing Shorty I hadn't imagined the whole thing. We passed the spot a few weeks later and Spags Belgiovani said, 'That's where Thommo shit himself and murdered a perfectly innocent bamboo thicket.'

But what they really rammed into us at Canungra was contact drills. We did them up yamas and down cliffs, across rivers and any other obstacle that would make our life a misery. There were contact drills for everything. 'Contact Front' when the forward scout opened fire. 'Contact Rear' if Charlie had a go at the tail-end. 'Ambush Left' and 'Ambush Right' if the enemy came from the sides.

We even practised contact drills in trucks. We'd be driving along some jungle track in an army truck packed in like sardines, rifles sticking up in the air to make more space for bodies, when suddenly some joker with blank ammo opens up on the vehicle from the bush with a machine gun. We then had to swing into contact drill pronto, which meant jumping from the moving truck to take up our defensive positions on either side of the vehicle, then lay down covering fire as the troops in the truck following us did a sweep to take out the machine gunner and whoever else represented the enemy.

It all sounded simple in the lectures but have you ever tried jumping from a moving truck seven feet above the ground with every bloke in the platoon trying to do the same thing at the same time with their rifle and bayonet, entrenching tool and machete and spare ammunition?

The driver, often as not, puts his foot on the accelerator in panic when the shots come, then jams on the brakes a moment later, or vicki-verka. You jump and hope for the best and collect a kick in the head from the bloke jumpin' behind you. Or the bloke in front of you jams his rifle butt into the difference between you and your sister. If you were real lucky you made it with only a couple of dozen nasty bruises and a fair amount of gravel rash.

At Canungra they drove us until we dropped and then thought of some way else they could persecute us. 'It's gunna be a lot worse when you useless bastards come up against Charlie, you're gunna die and they're gunna die laughing at your attempt to kill them!'

Because I was such a big bastard, 6'6" non-metric, they loved to have a go, 'Thompson, you big, dumb useless, uncut prick! The Viet Cong are going to drop to their knees and thank Buddha when they see you coming towards them!'

It went on like this all day and half the night as a regular army sergeant mouthed off at you. The worst part was that the bastard could do all the stuff that was breaking your heart and your bones and not even crease his jungle greens. There was a fast-growing agreement among us that the brown envelope wasn't such a shit-hot lottery to win after all.

Slowly we got the hang of this kind of soldiering and developed into something we'd never thought we could become. We became lean as a drover's dog, fit as a mallee bull and, most importantly, we'd learned to act and think for ourselves. It probably saved our lives a dozen times over in Vietnam. If there are three words that are sweet to the lips of any Vietnam vet it is them three – 'Contact bloody Drill'.

When we got to Vietnam we found that the Australians were the only force there who were jungle ready. Hardened to the fray.

And so to South Vietnam, Phuoc Tuy province and Nui Dat, the headquarters of the 1st Australian Task Force, 1 ATF for short. Nui Dat was situated in an old rubber plantation about twenty miles from a town named Baria. They called it the Funny Farm, because there was nothing funny about it. Just people in black pyjamas and conical hats who all looked and dressed the same, friend and foe alike.

These were a people who, during the dark of the night, would send seven-year-old children, mostly little girls, into the six-mile minefield we'd laid between the Horseshoe and the coast. The minefield was supposed to form a barrier that would prevent the VC, who were hiding in an area known as the Long Green, from getting to the villages and their rice fields.

Patrolling the boundaries of the minefield was the responsibility of a South Vietnamese infantry battalion and some Regional Force units. Not being the most interested soldiers in the world, they didn't bother. Now you might as well not have a minefield if you don't keep a careful watch over it. So these skinny kids, about the size of an Australian four-year-old, would sneak into the minefield at night. Their tiny feet and delicate sensitive toes were like little noses sniffing out the M16 jumping jack mines. They would shuffle along, their toes scraping the surface of the earth until they gently nudged the metal prong or side of the mine, trying to be so gentle so as not to set the mine off. Then the mine would be lifted and put someplace else they weren't meant to be so we'd be the ones to step on them next day.

Once in a while a truck which had been along Route 44 would report seeing bits of rag and broken flesh hanging on the barbed wire in the sunlight. Another seven-year-old had given her life for the Funny Farm.

It was getting late at the cafe and some of the blokes had fallen asleep. It had been a long day for all of us, it was time for beddy-byes in the pub. But there was one last thing. During the whole night Nam Tran hadn't said much. Every time I looked over at him he was nodding and smiling but he didn't say nothing. Then right at the end he stands up, he's pissed, but then we all are. He waves his tinnie around. 'You know why I come Australia?' he says.

'Yeah, so yiz can fuck us up like we done you blokes,' Animal shouts, his usual self, subtle as a smack to the side of the head.

The little man ignores him. 'I come because you fight good, same Vietnamese.' He means the Viet Cong, of course, not the South Vietnamese government mob. He looks around and I can see he wants to say more. 'Also, you bury our dead.' He taps his chest with his finger, 'You show me respect.' Then he sits down and stands up again almost immediately. 'In North Vietnam Army we say, "Walk without footprint, cook without smoke, speak without sound, move at night like a falling leaf."' Then he sits down and starts to cry.

I've never seen a Nog soldier cry, but I reckon he'll do me.

It's nearly two o'clock, time to get the mob up to the

pub for a good night's kip before tomorrow arvo, when we get the debrief on Shorty's bloody stupid idea. It's been a long day and I've got to get up early and clean the joint. I only pray there are no nightmares.

Chapter Three

I'm up at sparrow fart to clean up the cafe. It looks a bit like a mine has gone off inside the joint. I'd forgotten how many tinnies eleven blokes can drink in one sitting, because, of course, Bongface doesn't drink, though he's got through a fair few cans of Coke. They've, I mean we've, also polished off Shorty's plonk and there's cold chips, tomato sauce and bits of hamburger leftovers on just about every flat surface.

A broom and a mop, a bit of a wipe and a hose down where Animal's been sick out the back and, by the time Wendy gets in around eight o'clock, the place is ship-shape and ready to trade.

Three of the old-timers are in for their regular breakfast. They eat at Smoky Joe's and not at the pub because they've all had a blue with Willy McGregor some time in the past. As there is only one pub in town they're forced to drink his grog, but they're buggered if they're gunna give Willy a penny more than their thirst demands. Small towns are like that, forgiveness comes real slow.

Wendy feeds Anna and gets her mum up and into her wheelchair. The old chook is already grumbling but Wendy takes no notice, she's always cheerful around Anna and won't let the old girl spoil the day. First she does her mother's hair while the silly old bugger holds up a mirror and gives instructions. Struth, she's foreman material all right, can't help herself, she does bugger all except carp and criticise and I can hear her all the way downstairs as she has a go at Wendy. 'Yer never get it right, do you. You want me to look old, that's it isn't it, old and miserable!'

I hear Wendy laugh, 'Mum, you are old and miserable but I love you anyway.'

'That's what you say to me but what do you tell him, eh? Behind the door when you think nobody can hear!'

'Been sneaking up in your wheelchair, looking through the keyhole have you, Mum?'

'Humph! Don't think because I'm sick I can't hear. Nothing wrong with me ears, girlie.'

'What do you hear then?' I hear Wendy say, her voice still light.

'Never you mind. Plenty!'

There's a pause and I can imagine Wendy sighing. 'Half your luck, Mum, there's not a whole lot going on in our bedroom you couldn't tell in Sunday School.'

I can feel myself getting hot around the neck. She's right of course, I haven't made love to her in months and when I do it ain't exactly fireworks.

'Nanna says I'm sick because of Daddy,' I hear Anna shout out. 'Is that true, Mummy?'

'Mum! How dare you!' I can hear Wendy's anger. Then, 'No, darling, it's just something that happens sometimes in families. We're going to make you better.'

Now there is silence upstairs and I groan, stupid old bitch has gone and upset Wendy. She'll be real quiet when she comes down and when I ask, 'What's the matter?' she'll say, 'Nothing, it's just Mum.'

Then I hear Anna giggling and I know Wendy's plaiting her hair and tickling her under the nose with the fuzzy end of the completed plait before she asks Anna what colour ribbon she wants.

The old biddy will be sitting with her back turned to them feeding her face with a bowl of Cornflakes, milk dribbling down her chin. I wish she'd hurry up and die and leave us in peace. I wouldn't put it past her to leave her half of Smoky Joe's to the Anglican bishop instead of her daughter! Stupid old cow.

A commercial traveller comes in for breakfast and the usual assortment of customers wander in, most of them wanting cigarettes. It's almost nine o'clock before we can talk.

'How'd it go?' Wendy asks, 'Place looks spic 'n' span, you must have been up bright and early?'

My head's hurting and hammering against the side of me temples like the clappers of hell. There's something evil about a bad hangover, it hurts more three hours after than it does when you get up. Not that I'm not used to them, I've had more hangovers than most people have had hot breakfasts.

'Yeah, it was good,' I say, not wanting to give too much away. I'm not in a fit state or even ready to explain. I know I'm gunna have to level with her sooner or later, best try and get through the morning first. Perhaps even after the meeting, stall her until tonight when I know a bit more and my head hurts a bit less. 'Bit of a meeting this arvo at the pub, think you can manage here?' I say.

'Meeting? Another piss-up, you mean?'

'No, no! No grog. It's a fair dinkum meeting, love.'

'What about?'

'Look, I'll tell you later, okay?' I give her a look which says don't bug me now.

She sighs, 'Mum wanted to have her hair done at Hair to Stay.'

'Well, she can't.'

Wendy moves into the kitchen area and I follow her, I can see if anyone comes into the cafe. 'You go tell her that, Thommo. She's already made the appointment, it's a big thing, she's going to Mary Willow's seventieth.'

'Stiff shit,' I say, then instantly try to take it back, 'I mean, you explain it to her, she'll only have a go at me if I do.' But Wendy's heard me first off and won't stand for that kind of language. I can cuss, that's the way I am, but not directed at her or her mum.

'Stiff what?' she spits, 'Who do you think you're talking to, Thommo?'

'Look, it's real important, this meeting.' I try to keep my voice calm.

'Oh, I see. Important how? I thought last night was a party with your mates, "a grand reunion piss-up" is how you described it.'

'Yeah, well, it turned out to be more than that.' I've gone too far, said too much. I can see Wendy's not going to let it go.

'Thommo, what's going on? You in trouble? Your

82

mates? One of them? Stay away, we've got enough on our plate as it is.'

'Nah, nothin' like that.' I try to sound casual but I'm digging meself in deeper.

'What then?'

'Look, do me a favour. Leave off will ya, Wendy?'

She raises one eyebrow, she's a school teacher, or at least she was before Anna come along and she had to help run the cafe and care for her. I know that look. 'Secret men's business, is it?' she says, sarcastic.

Thank Christ, a customer walks in. I can't get over to him fast enough. Turns out he's not a customer, it's some bloke wants to flog me a new kind of ice-cream, pure fruit, nothing artificial, picked at dawn from an orchard in Queensland. Normally I'd give him the bum's rush. Nobody in this town eats anything that's good for them anyway, but now I treat him like a long-lost brother. I let him chat on about the crap he's flogging. I even take a large carton and the free scoop and a box of fancy cones. The salesman's stoked. I get the feeling sales haven't been that great. I turn around and Wendy's come out the kitchen and now stands behind the counter lookin' at me with her arms folded across her chest. Not a real good sign I gotta tell ya.

'I'm taking Mum to the hairdresser's,' she says, lips pulled tight.

One thing I've never done, about the only thing, is backhand her. Once I lost me block and took the Confederate and pushed the blade into her dressing-gown where her navel was. 'Go on, push,' she says real quiet, her eyes locked onto mine, 'Kill me and we'll both be out of our misery.'

I came so flamin' close to pushing the blade home that I start to tremble just thinking about it. Now I see me hand is half lifted to hit her. She and the kid are everything in the world I love, and all I've ever given her is grief. I sigh, and my hand drops to my side. 'Okay, we'll lock the cafe for the afternoon.'

'No,' she says, 'we need the money.'

'Well, suit yerself, I'm going to the meeting.'

'Right! Off you go then. Go on!' She points to the door.

'Right, screw yiz!'

'Right, that's it!' Wendy shouts. 'And don't bother to come back. Go pack your things!'

I'm real close to losing me block, 'What? You threatening me, Wendy?'

'I've had enough, Thommo.' Her eyes fill with tears. 'I can't take any more, mate.' She wipes both her eyes with the side of her fist, 'Mum and me own Smoky Joe's, just bugger off, will ya!'

'Shit. The meeting, it's for Anna!' I yell. 'The meeting's for Anna.' The words are hardly out of me mouth when I realise I've stuffed everything. I'm gunna have to tell her about last night right off.

'Anna?' Wendy looks hard at me. 'What about her?'

'Gettin' her better. A bone-marrow transplant.'

'Thommo, you better be very careful what you say next,' Wendy says quietly. Her voice is like ice.

'Yeah, well,' is all I can think to say.

The commercial traveller must have caught some of this, because I hear his chair scrape back. He gets up, folds his newspaper, 'I'll be off then,' he says. He's ordered coffee but I haven't brought it yet. He comes over to the counter to pay.

Wendy waves him away, 'That's all right. See you next time. Thanks for coming.'

I try to grin, apologise. 'Sorry, mate, bit of a domestic.' He walks out, not saying anything. I guess he's seen a few things in his time on the road.

The three old-timers have already et and gorn. They're all fast eaters. A plate of eggs, cuppa strong tea, four sugars, dash o' milk, a fag and they're off to wait for the pub to open.

I go over to the commercial traveller's table to clear the plates. He hasn't touched the fried tomato. I must buy a thousand uneaten tomatoes every year. 'Dead Toms' Wendy calls them.

Wendy starts to shut up the cafe. The doors are solid plate glass, no frames, they were her old man's pride and joy. He'd polish them every morning with a chamois kept special for the purpose. 'Same as on Woolworths in Narrandera,' he'd say to anyone passing by, tapping the shining glass with the knuckle of his forefinger.

He'd had 'Smoky Joe's Cafe' written in grey and white imitation smoke, the smoke writing curling across the two doors. He brought the Italian signwriter up from Griffith. Told him to go for his life, it has to be perfect, spare no expense, Mario Lanza. Being a musical man that's what he called all Eyetalians.

The stainless-steel bolts shoot home, one at a time, and it's Wendy and me alone. Shit, what am I gunna do?

'Now, what about Anna?' she asks.

'You better sit down, love,' I say, pointing to one of the tables. Then I tell her about last night. About Shorty's proposal. I'm expecting any moment to wear the heavy glass ashtray on the table. She don't say nothing, she's dead quiet, looking down, picking at one of her nails with t'other, her hands on her lap. Then, after a while, she looks up at me, a tear swells out her lashes and runs slowly down her cheek and onto her chin and drops. I don't see it land.

She sniffs. 'Anna's going to die, Thommo.'

'I know,' I say and suddenly I'm choked. We both know it, but we've never said it out loud. Every time we've got back from Sydney where we'd take little Anna to get a new dose of chemo at the Prince of Wales Children's Hospital in Randwick, we knew we weren't going to find a donor. Wendy's got no relatives to speak of and the Thompsons are just about died out in Currawong Creek. We're on a hiding to nothing trying to find an unrelated donor. But, until now, we've not admitted it to each other.

I look up and there's a couple of kids with their noses pressed against the doors lookin' in, wonderin' what's goin' on. Probably want to come in for a Paddle Pop. Anna's never going to grow up to do that or be a little brat like them two little buggers, dirty hand prints on Cec's precious plate-glass doors.

Then Wendy looks straight up at me, her blue eyes sharp, 'I'm coming to your meeting this afternoon,' she says.

'Jesus, no. No way!' I exclaim, surprised.

She rises. Standing, she's the same size as me sitting down. She stabs me in the chest with her forefinger. 'Thommo, I'm coming to that meeting or you can pack your things and bugger off. Go on, get going, on your bicycle.'

I've never heard Wendy swear except to say 'bloody', which ain't really swearin', and I'm dead shocked, she's done it twice in less than five minutes. I don't know what to say, because I can see she means every word.

'Anna's my child and I'm not prepared to leave her fate to a bunch of Vietnam vets who cry in their sleep!' she yells at me.

It's a blow well below the belt and she knows it. 'The Dirty Dozen?' she scoffs, 'That's real funny. Who are you then? Lee Marvin?' This really hurts, I know I'm a big, ugly bugger, but first Shorty and now her with the same crack.

I don't say nothing. I'm looking into my lap, thinking of something clever to say, my hangover is banging against me temples. I'm also trying hard not to do me block.

'We'll make it thirteen, The Baker's Dozen!' she says, sniffin'.

'Shorty won't buy it,' I say. 'The other blokes too. There's no way, love.'

'Stiff,' she says and grins at my surprised look. 'It's up to you now, Thommo.' She's got me fair and square. Nothing I can do. I'm gunna have to front Shorty and the boys. Bloody good thing, I think to meself. It was a stupid idea in the first place, might as well get it over with. Good piss-up last night and now we go our separate ways. Mo's dead, we're all loners anyway, Vietnam saw to that.

'Righto,' I say to Wendy, trying to play it light. 'Put the cat among the pigeons, eh?'

'Why not? A little pussy never did a bunch of blokes any harm,' she says.

I have to laugh, though I admit I'm a bit miffed, I mean, it's me wife talkin' dirty like this.

'Did you really mean for me, yer know, to piss off?' I say, trying to cover me embarrassment.

She nods her head.

'A man oughta belt you one.'

'Go ahead,' she says, 'You've done just about everything else.'

What can I say, it's true.

I go and see Shorty and we walk outside the pub and stand under a jacaranda tree. He hears me out, he's looking down at his boots, kicking the toe cap of his right foot into the fallen blossoms, exposing the soil under the purple carpet. He has his head to one side, his arms folded across his chest. Then he looks up, 'No way, Thommo,' he says quietly.

'Well, you'll have to count me out,' I say. 'Good piss-up last night, thank you.'

Shorty reaches up and grabs me by the shirt front, his head doesn't even come to the second button below me collar. 'Look, you big dumb bastard, we're trying to help you. Other vets too. Nam Tran says the Vietnamese kids are the same, only there's a lot more of them than us.'

I shrug, 'I know, mate, but Wendy is my life. Weren't for her I'd a topped meself a long time ago. She's given me an ultimatum, she comes in with us or she's leavin' me.' I shrug, 'Nothin' I can do, mate.'

He scratches his head, 'I dunno, Thommo.' He looks me in the eye, 'Bring a flamin' sheila in and there's bound to be trouble.'

Shorty has never married, 'There's enough Mafiosi in the world,' he's always joked. 'Give a grandson to my old man and he won't be happy until he's made the kid into the local Godfather.' He'd never take a bar girl in Vietnam neither. He must have pulled his pud to get some sort of relief, grog wasn't enough. Though I got to hand it to him, he knew how to get properly pissed. 'I don't want to tell me Catholic bride on our honeymoon that I've had the clap fifteen times.' But he's still single and he's got to be just about the best catch in the Riverina.

I stand there, lookin' stupid, saying nothing, now it's me kicking at the purple jacaranda blossom.

Eventually he sighs, 'We'll have to have a meeting before the meeting, it's not up to me to say, Thommo.' He looks up at me, squinting. 'You'll have to put the case to the boys, but I don't fancy yer chances, mate.'

'Fair enough,' I mumble. I'm hanging me big stupid head. I can see his point, I'd a done the same meself.

I get back to the cafe and tell Wendy.

'Thommo,' she says, 'Just understand, if they say no and you go on with it, you're out of my life. I love you, darling, but I'm not going to lose both you and Anna without being involved. Without having a say in the matter.'

'Wendy,' I say desperately. 'It ain't gunna work anyway. We ain't the blokes we used to be. We're all crook, we've got rashes and skin blisters and chloracne and the sweats, we're even scared to go to bed at night. Gazza was saying last night, and he wasn't on his own, when a helicopter goes over his house he dives under the bed. Look at us, Shorty, Bongface and Nam Tran are the only three who haven't got their gut hangin' over their belt like a sack of spuds. We're not The Dirty Dozen, we're a bunch of screwed-up Vietnam vets, we're drunks with nightmares, we've got Buckley's.' I look down at her, 'Pathetic, ain't it?'

'So, what are you saying?' she says fiercely, 'That you're not up to it?'

I look up, surprised. 'Well, yeah. The fuzz will be onto us in a flash. What the boys are proposing is against the law, flogging dope's illegal.'

'So smoking isn't?' she snaps back. 'You're having a fair whack at being on the wrong side of the law as it is.'

I don't have an answer. 'That's different,' I mumble, feeling stupid, 'A user and a dealer, that's not the same thing in the eyes of the law.'

'And what about Anna?'

I say nothing. Then I look at her. 'Wendy, it ain't gunna work. Don't you understand? We're past it. We're a bunch a hasbeens.'

She smiles, 'I'm going to make you a cup of coffee, Thommo. And then I'm going to tell you a story a young bloke once told me. A young man whom I loved, who wasn't afraid of anything.'

She gets up and I shout after her, 'Now, Wendy, don't start that shit!'

She brings me a cappuccino. I like it hot enough to burn my tongue, even though Spags Belgiovani says good Italian coffee should be warm and strong, too much heat and the flavour goes. He says that in Italy there are blokes who get sort of like a degree in coffee making, they're called baristas. Wendy puts it down in front of me, the steam rising through the brown speckled foam.

'This young bloke only told me once and I remember every word,' she begins. 'I'll tell it in my own words. Right?'

'Leave it off, Wendy!'

But she ignores me, 'There's big excitement at Nui Dat, Col Joye and Little Pattie are going to give a concert. The Americans have concerts quite often, but the Australians are not invited, this is the first time for the Australians. Their very own performers, Little Pattie is a real cracker and Col Joye a big star. D Company is in camp and the troops have been putting their spare greens under their mattresses to sharpen them up a bit. On the day they'll all shave a bit closer, comb their hair, clean their fingernails. They haven't seen a blonde in a miniskirt for over a year and their eyes are hungry.'

'Wendy, don't go there, mate!' I warn again.

She puts up her hand. 'Shush, Thommo!' I can see she's gunna go on and it's gunna hurt and it's not like her. She's stepping over our unspoken line and I don't know why. The coffee suddenly tastes like shit.

'On the seventeenth of August at 2.50 a.m. the VC mortar-bomb the base. About a hundred mortar shells and recoilless-rifle shells are fired. Quite a few are wounded, twenty-three I think, one soldier later dies. Most of the Task Force are stood-to in case there is a Viet Cong attack. They're not long at Nui Dat and the defences are not finished and they're expecting to see Viet Cong pouring into the base.'

Even though I'm far from happy with Wendy's bringing up all this past shit, I'm impressed at how she's remembered everything. I mean, how would a sheila remember a name like 'recoilless-rifle'?

'Your platoon is on duty minding A Company's perimeter whilst they are out on patrol. Those not on sentry at that moment were playing a crown-and-anchor game in the A Company headquarters and took no notice of the mortars, which were on the other side of the base. At the time you thought they were your own. The talk all night is of the concert party due in the day after tomorrow.'

'Wendy, why are you doing this?' I ask.

'You'll see,' she says. Her voice is quite calm but I can see her eyes, her big blue eyes are not smoky and soft like they usually are, they're hard, bright, like you can see the sharp little lights in them. She goes on. 'Well, the concert is on the eighteenth and it's still all anticipation among the troops. Then on the morning of the concert Harry Smith, your company commander, tells D Company you're going out on a routine patrol to relieve B Company, who'd gone out the previous morning to search for the enemy, follow them and, if possible, destroy them. The assumption is that the base was attacked by a small bombarding team of Viet Cong, who are well away by now.'

Wendy stops, then says, 'You can imagine how the blokes in your platoon feel. No concert, no Little Pattie in a miniskirt. It's the monsoon season and the leeches and every creepy-crawly in Vietnam is out for a taste of good red Aussie blood. You haven't been long back inside the wire anyway and you're pretty upset. Shorty tells your platoon that B Company's found a few VC mortar positions but hasn't engaged the enemy. It's a routine patrol and it's just bad luck D Company got the short straw.'

Wendy giggles. 'I remember you saying Animal tried

95

to throw a sickie. He claimed he'd sprained his ankle in the latrine. That way he'd be unfit for the patrol but would still be able to attend the concert.'

I can't help it and I laugh, 'Bongface asked him if he'd been using his toes to wank with! Animal has been telling half the camp for days what he'd personally like to do to Little Pattie if he could get her on her own for just ten minutes. It wasn't for repeatin' I can tell ya!'

Wendy's only heard me tell of this once, just after I got back from Vietnam. Animal, by the way, was no coward, he was a brave warrior who never shirked his share. It's just that in his priorities he always put pussy before valour.

Wendy continues. 'You slog through thick, tangled, wet scrub to the east. Every now and then you catch snatches of the Col Joye band warming up and you're none too happy. You relieve B Company, who are anxious to catch the concert.'

'Righto, that's enough!' I say to Wendy. 'Congratulations, I dunno how you've remembered all that shit and, what's more, I don't know what you think you're doing, love, but we're not going no further.'

Her voice is perfectly calm, but it's her school teacher's voice, 'I'll make you another cappuccino,

Thommo,' she says, rising from the chair. 'Don't move. Stay right where you are.'

She goes out back first then comes back to the cappuccino machine and soon enough she puts the coffee down in front of me. She also carries a tea towel under her arm and it looks as though she's used it to wrap something. Sitting down, she puts the bundle onto her lap. 'Now, where were we?' she says, smiling up at me all innocent like.

'Wendy, you know where. Just stop it, will ya!'

'Long Tan? Well, we've got to discuss it, Thommo.'

'No!'

'Yes.' She says it hardly above a whisper, looking straight at me.

'No, we bloody don't!'

'Thommo, I've been through the nightmares, the depressions, the days without speaking to me. Me waking up in the middle of the night and you're curled up like a baby weeping. You've hardly made love to me since Anna was born.' She stops and catches her breath, 'Now, I know you blame it all on Agent Orange, and you're right for some of the stuff that's going on. Anna also. But not all of it. Something happened at Long Tan, not just the battle, which was hell enough, but something else, something more personal. In your nightmares you scream about a machine gunner. "The machine gunner! The fucking machine gunner!" you yell out over and over and then you begin to weep like a small boy. What is it, Thommo? What happened, Thommo?'

I shrug, trying to stay calm, 'It's just stuff coming out, how do I know?'

Wendy is silent, then she brings up the dish cloth from her lap and puts it on the table and opens it. Inside is the medal I won at Long Tan. Then there's a light blue rectangle with the gold border about two or three inches long and about three-quarters of an inch wide. The last item is a little child's doll with Asian eyes.

The blue rectangle is the United States Presidential Unit Citation worn above the right-hand breast pocket. We were dead chuffed that the Yanks had given us a recognition for bravery. I can still remember the opening words of the citation:

By virtue of the authority vested in me as President of the United States and as Commander-in-Chief of the Armed Forces of the United States, I have today awarded the Presidential Unit Citation (Army) for extraordinary heroism to D Company, Sixth Battalion, The Royal Australian Regiment, The Australian Army.

D Company, 6th Battalion, was only the second

Australian army unit to be awarded the Presidential Citation, the first was to the 3rd Battalion Royal Australian Regiment for the Battle of Kapyang in the Korean War.

'What's this about?' I ask angrily, pointing at the stuff in front of her.

'Thommo, please tell me?' I can see she's about to cry.

'We won,' I say, real sharp. 'One hundred and eight men in D Company, most of us nashos, against 2500 North Vietnamese Army and VC troops and we won. That's all there is to know.' I point to the little blue ribbon, now I'm speaking sarcastic like, 'We were flamin' heroes, even President Lyndon B. Johnson, him of the "all the way with LBJ", said so.'

Wendy won't let go, 'Thommo, I know what happened at the Battle of Long Tan, it was our greatest victory in Vietnam. You *were* heroes, one and all.' She looks at me, her eyes pleading, 'What happened to *you* that day?'

Suddenly, looking into Wendy's sad blue eyes, I want to throw up, only it's a mental thing, like vomiting up fear and hurt and disgust. Without realising it, I have begun to talk, it doesn't sound like my own voice, more like a tape playing or some bloke reading from a book with me standing to one side, ready to interrupt if I want.

'We moved east from the base and eventually found enemy tracks that led into a rubber plantation. It's not like the jungle where you can see ten yards if you're lucky, where one man leads with the rest of the company following like a long snake. Here we can see 200 yards down the rows of young rubber trees. So the company breaks into open formation and it's not long before we get the order to disperse wide, two platoons up. Our platoon spreads out to cover a frontage of 150 yards or so with two of our sections up, including mine, in arrowhead formation. Shorty, along with our platoon headquarters and our third section, is fifty yards behind us. On our left is 10 Platoon in the same formation as us. Company HQ is 100 yards or so behind the lead platoons with 12 Platoon further back in reserve. We follow the direction of a well-worn track heading east-south-east.

'Harry Smith, our OC, knows what he's doing and we respect him big. He's trained us along Special Forces lines and we reckon we're the fittest, hardest and most disciplined company in Vietnam. In training we earned the name "Boots Company" because we could do fast, hard marches that left the others for dead. The hit song by Nancy Sinatra, "These Boots Are Made For Walking", becomes the unofficial D Company song. What's more, we're all mates willing to die for each other.' I sort of grin at Wendy, and my proper voice interrupts, 'Though perhaps not on this particular day, because there's a rumour going around that the concert party is to give another performance if we make no contact with the enemy and can get back in time the next day. It was bullshit, of course, but it keeps us in hope.'

It's funny, I've never talked about the eighteenth of August 1966 before, it's all been bottled up inside and now my voice is quite calm. Normally, just thinking about the day, I start to fall apart. Once I walked past a stand of bamboo in the local park and there must have been a bit of a breeze blow up so the bamboo creaked and I had a sudden panic attack. I mean, there wasn't any bamboo at Long Tan, it was a rubber plantation. But the bamboo was all the jungle patrols in Vietnam wrapped up in one and suddenly I was totally spooked at the familiar sound. I ran all the way home with my hands over my ears and hid under the bed. Now, in front of Wendy, this voice just keeps coming out of me, like I'm giving a debrief or a lecture or something.

'We're walking along and mine and Macca's section come to a road and we make a tactical crossing and move on into the plantation. So help me, unbeknownst to us in the forward section, a couple of minutes later a Viet Cong patrol comes strolling down the same road, chatting, happy as Larry. They're sandwiched neatly between our two front sections and the platoon head-quarters. Shorty is the first to see them and he opens fire with his M16, hitting one of them, and the rest dive into the rubber trees to the south-east.

'Up front we hear the firing and go to ground and wait to see what's happened. Mr Blunt, our platoon commander, comes forward and briefs me and Macca. He wants an extended line with a front of about 250 yards to go after the enemy.'

I look up at Wendy, explaining. 'You've got to understand, this is not a cautious approach, it's an aggressive formation, we're going after the buggers. The VC squad that walked into us may just be an isolated one or there may be a Nog camp in the area. We're expecting nothing we can't handle.

'Our going after the VC has placed us further away from 10 Platoon and the rest of the company. Shorty comes over and says to keep in the extended line but to change direction slightly so that we can move a bit closer.

'And then suddenly the shit hits the fan in a big way.

We cop heavy fire on our left flank and hit the deck fast where we manoeuvre to return fire. Chunks of bark are flying through the air, the latex running down the trunks of the rubber trees, striping them with these milky-white lines.'

I look up at Wendy again, 'Funny, how you notice dumb things like that. We can see nothing. The tracers are coming at us but there's nothing to fire at, just trees and the undergrowth concealing the enemy. Then I see a stream of tracers coming out of the top of the trees, like ten feet or maybe a little higher up. "Two o'clock up, the trees, about ten feet!" I shout to Mo, who's on my left, like always. We both fire into the thick rubber leaves and so help me, three Noggies fall out of the dark green canopy and if they'd been any deader when they landed they would've had to have been dug up.'

I hear Wendy laugh, but I don't look up at her.

'Then something happens we don't expect, Charlie starts coming at us in a direct assault, we can see them emerging from the bushes in good order. Jesus, we're the ones supposed to be the attacking force and suddenly we're going nowhere and they're coming at us. We hit them with everything we've got and they go to ground. But they keep firing at us, like they know what they're doing.

'After a while we settle down, holding our own. Thank Christ for Canungra, it's what all those contact drills have been about. If it's the VC, I tell myself, they'll have a go at us and then get out. That's their way, we'll just have to keep giving them curry and hang on a little longer.

'But this time they're here to stay. Suddenly the plantation ahead of us lights up like a Christmas tree. The first lot were just messing around, this second bunch coming at us . . . man, they're serious warriors. Then we realise it's the NVA, the North Vietnamese Army. Suddenly we're up to our eyebrows in excrement! They're attacking in extended line, the way we've been trained ourselves, about two yards apart, walking at a steady controlled pace and firing from the hip. It's straight out of the flamin' military manual.

'We knock down the first lot but the bastards keep comin', wave after wave. They're not the VC, not the black pyjamas, they ain't scared of us, these bastards know how to fight. The Asian hordes are upon us. As we cut each wave down, the survivors go to ground not too far to our front and continue to fire. It's only a matter of time and we're history.

'And then the platoon's right flank is attacked and our right-hand section is fighting for its life. The firepower coming in against us is awesome. Thousands of tiny green lights emerge from the rubber and the bush, most of it below knee height.

'We're on our bellies, there's no moving forward or, matter of fact, in any direction, anything more vertical than a leopard crawl and you're dead meat. We're taking casualties as we try to move to find the best cover. We've never been in anything like this before. But I've got to say it, the blokes are still identifying targets and yelling out the location. The noise is becoming deafening, even to be heard by the bloke next to you, you have to shout. It's amazing how much shouting goes on in a battle like this and I'm doin' me best to try to follow it and to direct the fire accordingly.'

I glance up, Wendy is looking at me, her eyes real soft and smoky. She looks like she's about to cry.

'It's about this time that Mr Blunt, our platoon commander, is killed while putting his head up to see where the artillery is landing so that we can call it in closer to us.

'Shorty takes over. I'm not aware of this at the time, I'm too busy trying to keep me own section intact, fighting the battle and attending to our casualties. It's the Australian way, you don't let a mate bleed to death for lack of attention, even in the heat of a battle.

'Then quite suddenly the rain comes, the way it does

in Vietnam. Nothing, then everything, the full monsoon. The sudden roar of the water even drowns the sounds of the fighting. It's coming down in solid sheets so we can't see more than about sixty or seventy yards. There's Noggies, dark shapes in the downpour, still spread out, in extended line and comin' for us. There's no way we can hold 'em, half our blokes are out of action and we're running dangerously low on ammo. It's all over, Red Rover.

'But then, as Lawsy once put it, "Cometh hope from the Heavens". We're stuffed five different ways and crucified twice over and our artillery, which seems to have taken forever to find its range, now hits spot on. They're dropping salvos just ahead of us. Even with the rain and the noise of battle we can hear the beautiful whistle of the shells. Then the ripping sound, like the air being torn apart, is followed by a blue flash. *Kerboom*! Suddenly there are Noggies being blown sky high, limbs hurled through the air, screams, headless, armless, legless torsos rolling, flying, somersaulting, bouncing, sliding in the mud. Talk about just in time!

'But the bastards only stop for a moment.

'By now the rubber plantation is just mud and tracer bullets kicking up same, with the rain competing for attention. The VC are yelling blue murder. It's weird, but you can hear the human voice through just about anything. They're going ape-shit as they come at us, jumping over low bushes, running straight, keeping formation, firing from the hip. Who was it trained these bastards?

'Our artillery is now coming in real heavy and real close. There's wholesale slaughter in Charlie's ranks, but you could've fooled me, they're still advancing, the bastards must be high on something.

'We've been going about an hour and a half and finally, we, I mean, our artillery, get the better of them and we bring them to a halt, but the enemy fire is still heavy. By this time, I reckon half our platoon is dead or seriously wounded.

'With the frontal assault halted for the moment I now see a Noggie machine gunner's got our range. In the heat of the battle I should've seen him, but I didn't. I only see him when he takes out Maloney, who has moved to help out McKenzie, who's wounded. I crawl over, they're both dead.

'The VC machine gunner puts a line of tracers no more than eighteen inches ahead of Mo and me, the mud the bullets kick up splattering our greens. I have a rough idea where the firing is coming from, I try to get what's left of the section to concentrate their fire in the direction. But it doesn't work. Either I've got the direction wrong or he's got real good cover which gives him the confidence to keep havin' a go at us.

'The machine gunner has to be stopped or he'll kill us all. He can be got at from the left but our blokes are all dead or wounded out there. We're pinned down like bugs in a museum and he knows it.

'Being run over by the Asian hordes, sheer numbers, is one thing. Being taken to the New Jerusalem by a Noggie machine gunner and his mates is quite another. A disgrace. Not on.

'The artillery is still coming in magic. It's landing so close that the Noggies out the front of us who are not pulverised are putting their heads down as the salvos are about to land. I notice that even the machine gunner stops firing as the incoming salvo screams down and hits and he doesn't start again for a good few seconds after the blast.

'Just as another salvo hits I shout to Mo, tell him what I'm gunna do and instruct him to stay put, to get the blokes to give me whatever covering fire they can. He nods and puts up his thumb. The racket is something terrible and me throat is hoarse from shouting.

'I've spotted what looks like a hollow in the ground. Unfortunately it's within a small clearing with no rubber trees for protection, but it's in just the right spot to take out the Viet Cong gunner, that is if I can get close enough.

'I wait for the next salvo. I hear the whistle and the scream as it is about to land. I'm on my knees and elbows digging dirt, into the mud and slush, staying flat to the ground as the salvo lands, moving towards the hollow.

'I hope like hell the machine gunner and his mates have their heads down, I'm expecting any second to be blown apart. The salvo lands. The rain is still pissing down as I slide sideways into the hollow, it's half filled with rainwater and I send up a huge muddy spray. I'm safe. I'm lying in eight inches of water, but I'm safe. Then the machine gun starts up again. The bastards have picked up my movement and there's bullets spraying every which way. I'm grinning, old Thommo is safe in his ditch, snug as a bug in a rug. Then I see it's not me they've picked up on, it's Mo, he's coming at me, sliding across the mud. The dip in the ground isn't big enough for both of us and when he sees this and stops his slide he's more exposed than ever. The machine gun is kicking up mud everywhere. Mo takes up a firing position in the open beside me.

'"Oh, Jesus, no!" I scream, then Mo's head explodes and isn't there any more. Warm blood spurts from his neck in an arch, two feet high, landing on my back and neck. It feels warm. The muddy water I'm lying in turns crimson. The rain is still beating down.

'"Oh no! Oh, Jesus, Mo's dead! The machine gunner! You fucking arsehole! The Nogmachinefucking*gunnerrr*!" Something slides down my cheek and splashes into the water and bobs up again. It's Mo's eye, attached to membrane, floating in the blood and rain-pocked water.

'I'm losing it fast. But somehow I've got the instinct to wait for the next salvo coming in. I can hear it coming. It's like I'm riding the shell myself. I'm riding the salvo piggy-back. I only want to live as long as it takes me to kill the machine gunner. Nothing else matters. The salvo lands with a deafening roar and seems to be right next to me with the shrapnel whistling over my head. "Please God don't let me get killed before I get to him," is all I can think. I scramble towards the machine gunner, the rain battering my face. I'm within fifteen yards and his head ain't up yet. I've got a grenade in my hand and I've pulled the pin out and used up a couple more seconds before I throw it. I can now see where the machine gun is and I prop and lob it perfectly.

'This is the first time I realise I won't make it back. Nobody could, leastwise a big bastard like me. I'm flinching as I scramble away, expecting any moment to feel the bullets ripping into me. The grenade explodes, maybe it will keep the enemy from firing elsewhere just a few moments longer. I go for it, crouching, head down, legs pumping, hands clawing the mud. I'm not dead yet, though I should be. The air is full of every kind of deadly shit again, tracers whipping past me. I slide the last few feet, boots first into the hollow. This time a great scarlet sheet splashes up out of the scooped-out earth. The artery in Mo's neck is now pumping a three-inch arc, a spent pipe. The machine-gun post is silent. I lie in the hollow howling like a dingo. "Gotcha! Mincemeat! Fucking hamburger!"'

Now my own voice is back and I can feel the shakes beginning. I fight it, I fight back the panic.

Wendy reaches out and grabs my hand and holds on tight as I start to sob, 'Mo's dead.'

I turn to Wendy, 'We've made this pact, see.' I pull up my sleeve to show her, though she's seen it thousands of times. 'The tat on me arm of the M16 with "Mo" wrote on the butt, he's got one exact the same with "Thommo" on his.' I've never told her that. 'Two warriors never to be parted.' Now I'm blubbing like a kid.

Wendy pulls me hand up to her lips and kisses it, 'Go on, Thommo, get it all out,' she whispers. I can sense there's tears running down her face but I can't see them, my eyes are turned inwards somewhere I don't want to look.

Now I'm sobbing and out of control. I can't hold meself together no more. Wendy is standing behind me and has her arms about me. 'I'm a bloody coward. Oh shit, what am I gunna do? I'm a heap o' shit. They give me a medal. I let me best mate die, took the ditch for meself and they give me a fucking medal! A lousy medal.'

Dimly I can hear Wendy shouting my name. 'Thommo! Listen to me, Thommo!' She's kissing me on the eyes and the cheeks and screaming out. 'Thommo, listen to me, mate!' Her voice is suddenly hysterical and it cuts through, 'Hear me, you bastard!!'

I stop whimpering and I hear her say, 'You told Mo to stay, to cover you. He disobeyed. It wasn't your fault. You killed the machine gunner and God knows how many others.'

'The noise, he didn't hear me. He must've thought I said to come, be my cover, me and him together, like always. I should've died with him. There was no chance I'd survive, I was good as dead after I'd used the grenade. Oh, Jesus, why didn't I die.'

'Thommo, I love you, I'm proud of you.' Now she's

sobbing, her arms around me neck, her head against my back, her shoulders heaving.

Later, after I've had a couple of stiff shots and Wendy, who doesn't normally drink, has had a nip of Scotch as well, she reaches out and picks up the doll and stands it upright on the table. The little Vietnamese doll dressed in national costume makes it seem like it was a thousand years ago and, then again, like it happened yesterday. She smiles, her eyes are still red from blubbing, but they're smoky again, then she nods towards the little doll, 'Anna's medal, tell me the story again.'

I try to laugh, glad to come away from where we've just been. The doll story is one of the few things I have told her about Vietnam. But now, with the story at the back of my mind, I can talk about the stuff I couldn't before.

'There's a whole lot more that happens towards the end of the day. Shorty gives the order to pull out and Animal shouts, "Thommo, get the fuck outta there, we're moving out."

'I get lucky and scramble over to him, mostly on my elbows and knees, then we're off like jack rabbits, zigzagging, hoping for the best, Nog bullets stinging the air around us. I suddenly see yellow smoke through the rubber and grab Animal by the arm and pull him over. "D Company!" I shout, "That's our smoke."

'But it isn't, it's 12 Platoon who've been trying to find us and have taken a hiding themselves. Thirteen of our platoon finally make it back to them. We don't even have time for a fag when the VC come at us again. We get the hell out of there, fighting as we go, and eventually link up with D Company who've been fighting pretty hard themselves. The rain is still pissing down.

'Twelve Platoon tell us the company is two hundred yards to the north and they're going to try to join them. We leave a rear party of seven blokes behind to cover us and taking 12 Platoon's dead and wounded with us we get the hell out of there. We get to the company position with the rear party making it soon after. We're home and hosed, but as it turns out it is more like out of the frying pan into the fire. The rest of D Company have been fighting pretty hard and, like us, they're just about out of ammunition. But at least we're back together again. There's a bit of a lull in the battle and we can only hope that the next Charlie assault can be contained.

'But then the VC stop to regroup and something wonderful happens, a Huey helicopter arrives and drops boxes and boxes of ammunition. Even in the rain it must have been seen and heard by the enemy and the miracle is that it wasn't shot out of the air.

'Yet the VC come again, we've got plenty of ammo but we're outnumbered ten to one and they're good soldiers one and all. Again, it's only a matter of time.

'But just like a John Wayne movie when it's all over bar the shouting, the cavalry arrive, A Company in armoured personnel carriers equipped with 50-calibre machine guns and they come straight into the attack. Then some of B Company come in from the west. By the time darkness comes we've driven the enemy off. It's still coming down in buckets.

'Eventually the whole group moves back to the edge of the plantation and deploys to defend a piece of ground big enough and clear enough for the dustoffs to land. We form a defensive square around it with the APCs at each corner armed with their 50-calibre machine guns.

'The dustoff choppers come in, it's a night operation and very risky but the fly-boys do the job, taking all the wounded and dead out, that is all except those who were left behind from our platoon. There's no going back into that battlefield in the dark and finding our dead will have to wait until morning when, I tell myself, I'm gunna go back and fetch Mo Jacka.

'About 1 a.m. the last dustoff leaves and we get the chance to settle down and wait out the night, all of us are pretty certain the Viet Cong and the NVA are gunna be back. But at least there's time for a brew-up and then, if we're lucky and our nerves will allow us, an hour or so of shut-eye.

'It's still raining.

'Next morning the battalion advances in the rubber plantation again, but we're riding on tracks. The tracks advance real slow, expecting enemy contact any moment. All the boys want to do is reach our platoon dead and I want to get to Mo's body and cover him with my hutchie before anyone else sees he's got no head. There's far worse sights among the enemy dead, but it don't seem decent somehow for them to see a mate and a member of our platoon like that. I know it's stupid to say, but it would have embarrassed Mo.

'We're coming up to our platoon battlefield when we see Ocker Barrett leaning against a tree and in bad shape, he's got his hands in his lap and from the waist down he's soaked in blood. His hands look like two lumps of raw meat. "What took you so fucking long?" he asks. I had to fight back the tears but when we reach the platoon battlefield I lose it completely, the other blokes as well. There they are, our dead brothers, lying in an arc, still facing the enemy, most of them holding their rifles in a firing position. They've been washed clean by the rain and they look as though an order from Shorty would bring them back to instant life. I pull myself together and then lose it again as I come across Bongface, he's badly wounded but he's alive. God's given us two of our boys back. I call the MO over. "You okay, mate?" I say to Bongface, still crying. It's a stupid question, but he half opens his eyes and his big smile comes on and I know I love him. The MO takes over and gives him a shot of morphine.

'Then I run ahead, I've got my hutchie out and it's flapping as I run, I can see where Mo is lying and come up to him and spread the hutchie on the ground beside him and roll him onto it. Rigor mortis has set in and one leg sticks out and I take off my webbing belt and wrap it around both legs and pull the stiff leg against the other and tie it down. I wrap Mo up and tie him tight and now only I know what's underneath as the chopper lands to take him away forever. I'm bawling like a kid now. I can hear the dustoff coming in to take our dead and wounded. It's right above me. It's going to land in the same clearing as Mo and me. A single yellow bamboo leaf, shaped like the head of a Zulu spear, was stuck to the heel of Mo's left boot. I rushed forward as the dustoff lifted him up from the ground, the chopper blades above my head a wind-rush of cool air in the humidity, and grabbed the leaf off his heel and shoved it into the pocket of my greens.'

Wendy is hugging me and comforting me. 'It's okay, mate, it's okay, let it all come out,' she soothes me. She's kissing me and I can feel her soft lips on my wet cheeks.

After a while I pull myself together and go on. 'D Company lost seventeen men, thirteen from our platoon. But Charlie paid a bigger price, we buried 245 of their dead on the battlefield and we captured three wounded. Later VC records taken by the US Forces showed that the total enemy losses at Long Tan were 500 dead and 750 wounded.'

I look at Wendy, 'Which, I admit, is a long way around to get to the story of the little Vietnamese doll.'

'No, Thommo, you've no idea how much it helps. Do you want to talk about Mo?' Wendy asks gently.

'Nah, I've said all I can. No sense goin' further.' I point to Anna's medal, 'Now, about the doll.'

'Yes, the doll,' Wendy smiles, encouraging me, 'Tell me the story again.'

I'm on a bit of a roll and I want to get all the shit off my liver in one go. 'Are you sure? I mean, I've told you the doll bit before?'

'Never like today, Thommo. The doll is now a part of the whole story. I see it quite differently to before.'

I laugh at the thought of the doll. 'Righto, then.' I blow my nose and take a breath to get started again, crying is no good for a bloke's self-respect. 'Lemme see now. Okay, we've done a pretty good battle and the South Vietnamese government want to give some of us who fought at Long Tan one of their medals for gallantry. So back at Nui Dat a medal parade is organised with all the top brass to be in attendance. Then, at the last minute, the Australian government puts the kybosh on the medal. They point out that no Australian combat soldier may receive a foreign military decoration without approval from the Queen. Bloody stupid I know, but there you go.

'Now it seems because of this decision the South Vietnamese government are about to lose face, which, in Asia, is a very big deal and to be avoided at all cost. It's your classic Mexican stand-off. The parade can't be cancelled and the medal ceremony can't be conducted.

'Then someone in their government comes up with the dolls, the Vietnamese dolls. Buggered if I can see the logic, but then who knows how the Asian mind works. We're to get one of these dolls instead of a medal, though some of the heroes got cigar and cigarette cases.

119

We discover there's some sort of pecking order goin' on here. The medal we're supposed to receive is called The Cross of Gallantry, which, it turns out, has three orders, Palm, Silver Star and Gold Star. The palms get a cigar case, the silvers get a doll and the golds get a cigarette case. We're expected to take all this dead serious, like it's a huge honour, a group of warriors back from hell, most of them clutching a child's doll. Then Animal shouts from the back. "The least you lousy buggers could've done was make it a blow-up!"'

Wendy and me have a bit of a laugh together. Then she's dead serious. 'Thommo, you're to take the doll with you, take Anna's medal today. Tell Shorty you've got a female in your presence, whether the boys like it or not, that she's been with them since after Long Tan. Then hold up Anna's medal for them to see. If they say no to The Baker's Dozen, to me coming in, then don't bring the doll back.' Wendy stops and looks directly at me. 'And don't come back yourself, you hear, because that will mean you're married to the wrong doll.'

Chapter Four

Now I can't exactly say the excrement hit the rotating blades when I attend Shorty's preliminary meeting. The hangover factor comes into play and I don't think the audience can take in the implications all that well. Shorty, as usual, opens the proceedings without too much pre-chat.

'Thommo wants his wife, Wendy, in on the act,' he announces.

This is followed by total silence. It is not what you'd call 'stunned silence', more like the fact that the information they have just received is sinking in very bloody slowly.

From the look of the bloodshot eyes surrounding me, the combined drumming going on in their heads would put a hard rock concert to shame. All except Bongface of course. Even Nam Tran looks a little under the weather, though it's hard to tell looking into your basic Nog face.

Willy McGregor has given us the upstairs sitting room and put out chairs from the dining room downstairs. I guess he reckons we've paid our way and he's well ahead on the cash register, after which a bit of old-fashioned courtesy can't do no permanent damage.

'Huh? Say again?' Ocker Barrett finally grunts and shakes his head, then realises this is a big mistake and holds his head in both hands, groaning.

Animal is the first to speak properly. 'Shit, I need to throw up,' he says and leaves the room in a half crouch, one hand on his belly. I hope to Christ he knows where the upstairs Gents is or Willy ain't gunna let me forget this day for the rest of me flamin' life.

Then Killer Kowolski says very slowly, 'I don't believe I've heard what I've just heard, have I?'

Even Flow Murray, who'll agree to anything, is silent.

It takes Bongface to make the first bit of sense. 'Thommo, I ain't got nuthin' against your woman, mate. I ain't even met her, but there's things men does and things sheilas does. This is . . .'

'Secret men's business?' I say, repeating Wendy's earlier crack.

Bongface gives me a look, 'You sendin' me up, Thommo?' I can see he's not too happy, thinking I'm having a go at him being an Abo.

'Naw, mate, it's just what Wendy, me wife, said when I told her the boys ain't gunna buy the proposition.'

Bongface relaxes and gives me his big smile. There's definitely something to be said for staying off the piss.

'Well then, that's it, ain't it, mate?' Spags Belgiovani says, relieved and obviously pleased the unpleasant business is over. ''Cause your wife's dead right, it is men's business.'

'It's not that easy,' Shorty cuts in. 'If we don't let her in, Thommo's out. She's told him to piss off out of her life if we don't agree.'

'Shit, hey?' Macca says. I can see he's impressed. 'She don't bugger around, do she?' The others look a bit shocked but don't say nothing.

It's then that I remember the Vietnamese doll. I've put it into a plastic bag and placed it at my feet. I pick the bag up and get up off my chair. 'Look, fellas, gimme a break, will ya? I'm between a rock and a hard place, it's not my idea. Wendy says there's always been a woman looking after us. That is, since Long Tan.' I take the doll out of the bag and hold it up for all to see. 'It's sort of our, you know, good-luck symbol.'

'Talisman?' Lawsy says.

'Yeah, that also.'

Then they all begin to laugh.

'Fuckin' doll,' Animal says, re-entering the room. He wipes his mouth with the back of his hand and points at the Vietnamese doll. Though I don't know whether he means it's good or bad or even knows what we've been talking about. Probably not.

'Wendy says to ask you blokes, by the way, she's a school teacher, she says to ask you to put up your hands if you've kept your doll?' I raise the little doll above me head again and give it a bit of a shake.

Nothing happens for a moment then slowly everyone's hand goes up, 'cept Bongface's and Shorty's.

'I got a fag box,' Bongface says, and you can tell he's disappointed, even though it's the highest of the three decorations. Shorty don't say nothing, though I now remember he got a cigarette case as well.

'There you go!' I say, not quite knowing what I mean. Except I feel suddenly that the situation's not entirely hopeless. Though with my grog-addled brain, it's not one I care to trust all that much.

Well, there's a lot of toing and froing and up and downing and chewing the fat and private conversations going on with the bloke in the chair next to you. Then

Shorty finally shouts the room to silence. 'Righto, we ain't getting nowhere, gentlemen. Thommo, do you think Wendy would come around and address this meeting? Tell us why she reckons we should count her in on the scam?'

To everyone's surprise Nam Tran now stands up to speak. Nobody's stood up 'cept me. They've all just stayed put and talked from their chairs. 'Women very important Viet Cong,' he says and then promptly sits down again.

I look over at Shorty and nod, 'Yeah, I reckon she'd come.'

'It doesn't mean she's in, you understand?' Shorty says, anxious to get it straight. 'Just that she'll know she's had a fair hearing an' all.' He looks around and then back at me, 'Okay, mate?'

The boys all nod and mumble their approval. I can see they don't want to upset me by coming straight out and refusing. It's like Shorty's rescued them from an embarrassing situation and they're grateful.

I nod back at Shorty. 'Be about half an hour, maybe a little longer.'

Shorty smiles, 'Righto then, that'll just give us time for a deeply cleansing ale, pub will be open by now.' The chairs scuffle backwards on the polished jarrah floor. Boys can't get to the bar downstairs quick enough for the 'hair of the dog' and I wish I was goin' with them.

I catch Gazza's eye as I'm going out and I can read what's going on in his head clear as daylight. He's shaking it slowly from side to side and what he's saying inside is, 'Jesus, Thommo, you oughta belt her one. I wouldn't put up with that kind a shit from my missus!'

I admit, I'm not much meself, but I'm glad I don't wear Gazza's head atop me shoulders. He's a good warrior but he has his moments. After Vietnam he joined the French Foreign Legion, which scrambled his brains even further.

Macca puts his hand on my arm as I go through the door, but he don't say nothing. He's a good bloke, Macca. Like Mo, not much said, but always there at your side when you need him.

I know Wendy will want to doll herself up a bit and, as every bloke knows, that takes a bit of time. I'm kind of grinning to meself as I walk down the street on the way to Smoky Joe's. These dumb bastards don't know what they just agreed upon. Wendy Thompson ain't a woman to be denied. Besides, she's not got a brain freshly fumigated by last night's piss fumes.

It don't take too long to get Wendy to the meeting. She worms her way into a pair o' fresh jeans by lying on the bed and pulling them up over her bum, wriggling and puffing like she's fitting on a new skin.

'Hey, you've got no panties on,' I say, pointing to the unzipped jeans. She's lying there, topless, looking beautiful, and I'd be telling a lie if I said I didn't feel a stirring.

'Don't fuss, Thommo, panties would show through, it's the new look. Now help me with the zip, will ya?'

'Jesus, Wendy, them jeans are so tight if I zips ya, it'll cut a very painful path through the jungle!'

She laughs. 'That's why I need you, Thommo. I need both my hands to push down my tummy to avoid just such an eventuality!'

'I suppose a quickie would be out of the question?' I ask, hopefully.

'What!' she yells and stabs a finger down at her jeans, 'And have to do this all over again! Get real, lover boy, I'm dressing for a different sort of action.'

'Take a deep breath then,' I instruct. Then I zip her, successfully missing the forest canopy. She slips on a light blue sweater that's not exactly flat in the front nor sagging neither. She ain't that big in the front but her nipples point to the moon and there's as nice a handful available as any man could wish for. I admit the look ain't exactly what you'd call subtle and a married bloke like me ought to say something as a matter of duty. But after this morning I'm not game to open me big mouth. Besides, to tell the truth, I'm concentrating on fighting the battle of the bulge down in me own jungle region.

Thank Gawd, she don't put on high-heel boots but slips on her loafers. Then she slaps on a bit of lippy and some blue stuff around the eyes, grabs her handbag and a shopping bag. I wonder why she needs the bag and she sees me looking at it. 'Gotta go to the chemist on the way back,' she says and we're ready to go.

Wendy's a real good sort. She'll turn any head in the street, even other birds look at her. The young jackaroos in from the bush hang around the pavement and wait until I go out the back before they come into Smoky Joe's, just so they can be served by her. Not just the young ones neither, the rice-a-risos from the irrigation area and the cow cockies too. She could've had anyone she wanted and the poor little bugger landed up with me. When the two of us are together somewhere, you can see it in the eyes of the blokes, they're wondering how come a big ugly bastard like me managed to get a cracker like her?

Wendy's got this natural blonde hair, it's not like

your canary yellow, sort of tawny, cut short in what she calls 'a bob'. It's dead sexy, even if I say so meself. Having Anna hasn't changed nothing and she's slim as a twig and her bum is firm as two tennis balls kissing.

I'm well aware she's probably dressed a bit over the top for the meeting. Most of the blokes are in thongs and stubbies, Animal's not even wearing a T-shirt, though he's carrying that many tattoos it looks like he's got on some sort of fancy hairy garment. On the other hand, Wendy don't do too much she ain't thought about first. Like she don't normally go on display and I can't help feeling she's been expecting me to come and fetch her all along.

The jeans were spread out on the bed when I come in and also the sweater. She's got her mate, Brenda Hamill, visiting. Brenda sometimes serves in the cafe, so we don't even have to close down for the arvo. The old cockatoo can look after Anna and if there's any problem Brenda knows what to do.

I tell meself I don't deserve a bird like Wendy. If she tells me to get outta her life it'll take her about ten minutes to find another bloke a whole heap better than yours truly. Christ, I love that little bird so much it fucking aches.

We get to the pub and Wendy tells me to wait on,

she needs to go to the Ladies. Why do chicks always have to enter every toilet they pass? She comes out a couple of minutes later and I can't believe me eyes, she's wearing these black boots. The heels are about six inches high and the tops come to just below her knees. She sees the expression on my face and puts her finger to her lips, stops me saying something I ought.

'It's the new look,' she says, grinning. 'C'mon, let's go, lover boy.'

Well, maybe it was Shorty's cleansing ale, or Wendy's entrance that does the trick. Suddenly the whole room is alert and I can see the boys are eating her up with their eyes. Why shouldn't they, I'm doing the same meself and she's the piece of pie in me own pantry.

Shorty is still playing sergeant and now he clears his throat. 'Okay, fellas, settle down now!' He's already met Wendy and knows she's a doll, on the other hand he's never seen her geared up like this. He clears his throat again. 'Gentlemen, huh, this is Wendy, Thommo's wife, make yerselves known by name starting from the back.'

Each does the same, sort of half standing up and saying their name. They get a smile from Wendy they're gunna dream about in private later on. Animal can't conceal his feelings and is already droolin' at the mouth.

'Well, yeah,' Shorty says, looking sort of sideways and downwards, not actually at my wife, 'Wendy, I've got to be honest, the boys here, well, ah, they're, you know, not all that keen on what Thommo says you've asked.'

'And you?' Wendy asks, putting Shorty on the spot.

'Well, yeah, me too,' he mumbles.

'I don't blame them.' Wendy turns and smiles at Shorty, 'Or you, Sergeant di Maggio.' Then she looks around with this serious expression. 'I didn't fight in Vietnam. Or witness my mates die. You've been together a long time. Why should you trust a civilian? I wouldn't if I was in your place.'

That's bloody clever. She don't say, 'Why should you trust a woman?' So now all present can save face. We're not bird-bashin' or nothin' like that, just being ourselves, Vietnam vets not trusting no one but our own kind.

Wendy flashes me a smile, 'If Thommo's anything like the rest of you, you don't even have any civilian friends. Nodding acquaintances maybe, but not what you'd call a trusting male relationship outside a veteran.' She looks about and it's obvious she's hit a home run. Now she kind a grins, but it's sort of sad. She looks down at the floor, and then up through her lashes sideways, 'It's no secret that living with a Vietnam vet isn't easy.' She is silent a moment as though she's thinking how she should say something, then she says, 'A veteran's wife is also a veteran, also a victim of the Vietnam war. What she's definitely *not* is a civilian.'

She says this real quiet. The boys laugh, but it's not funny like it's a joke she's made. I can tell they're tuning onto her wavelength pretty damn fast. You can see they're thinking, 'This chick understands us, she knows what it's like.'

'Well, yes, Mrs Thompson,' Lawsy says from the back of the room, 'that's not precisely the same thing, is it?' We all turn to look at him. 'We only trust those who've gone through the same experience. Who have been to Vietnam as a soldier.'

I hold me breath, Wendy's not gunna stand for that. Lawsy's another of the single blokes amongst us and maybe he doesn't know what the women have to go through. But Wendy doesn't take exception.

'Only trusting your own kind, that's both a strength and a weakness, Mr Laws,' she replies. If Lawsy wants to be a pain in the arse by calling Wendy Mrs Thompson, she's gunna give him as good as she gets.

'How come a weakness, Wendy?' Shorty interrupts.

'Well, the strength is what Mr Laws says,' Wendy says, looking at all of us except Lawsy. 'You trust each other completely and that's good.' She looks over at Shorty, 'The weakness is that you will be operating in an environment you don't understand. The civilian environment. If Thommo's typical, in all the years since Vietnam you've never really settled down, have you? Now you're about to operate a giant scam, a very delicate one at that, and you're going into another sort of jungle, the civilian jungle.' She stops and looks around. 'And you're unarmed and badly prepared.'

Lawsy ain't through with her yet. 'I thought you said you weren't a civilian, that wives are veterans as well?'

It's a good point and I can see some of the boys are smiling. Lawsy's got this sort of half grin on his gob, like he's cross-examining her in a court of law.

'Ah, but I'm a veteran who never got lost in the jungle, Mr Laws.'

'And what exactly does that mean?' Lawsy asks. I think he's beginning to enjoy himself.

The sunlight from the window is behind Wendy and her hair is like a golden halo. 'Mr Laws, with the greatest respect, it is well known that your law practice in Griffith is a revolving door for both staff and clients. It's not that you're not a brilliant lawyer, because your reputation precedes you. It's because you have all the problems of a Vietnam vet. In other words, like Thommo, you're operating in an alien environment. Not a very big one either, Griffith is hardly the big smoke.' She pauses, 'Or don't you agree?' Wendy says, smiling at him.

'Bugger me!' Spags whispers next to me, 'She's right about Lawsy!'

Lawsy half rises, he's a bit red in the face. Christ, it's gunna be on for one and all and, frankly, I think me wife's gone too far this time, stepped way over the mark. You can't humiliate a bloke in front of his mates like that.

But Lawsy suddenly grins, 'Wendy, I'm sorry, please call me Lawsy. Perhaps it would be a good idea to start all over again?'

'Of course!' Wendy says, smiling. 'And I'm sorry about the crack about the revolving door.' She gives him a sunburst from her pearlies that fair nearly knocks us out of our chairs.

'Jesus, Thommo, you've got one out of the box there, mate,' Macca whispers.

'No, Wendy, please don't apologise, you're right,' Lawsy continues. 'What you said about me and my law practice is true.'

None of us vets has ever seen Lawsy eat crow.

He's the brains in our mob. I've got to hand it to him, what he's said wouldn't be easy for any bloke to say to a girl.

'I think she's right about us,' Flow suddenly announces. 'I vote Wendy in.'

Goddamn, Flow! Not now, not yet! An endorsement from Flow Murray at this point would just about screw everything up.

Thank Christ, Shorty ignores him and takes over again. 'If you're right and, as you claim, we don't understand the civilian jungle, and I'm not saying you are, then why would bringing you in help us?'

Wendy brushes her hair back with a flip of the hand. Now she looks deadly serious. 'Shorty, all I've got to go on is what Thommo told me this morning. That you propose to grow dope and sell it for the benefit of veterans' children who have suffered from birth defects as a result of Agent Orange. I am deeply grateful that you have decided Anna, our child, should be the first recipient.' She pauses and looks at him, 'Is what I've said correct so far?'

Most of us nod, 'Yeah, fair enough,' Shorty grunts, looking down at his boots.

'Well, then, before I answer your question, I'd like to ask you all a few questions,' she says real polite and then sort of half smiles. It's her dangerous smile and I'm glad the rest don't know it. 'May I?' Wendy asks.

'Fire away,' Macca says. I can see he's seriously in love with me wife.

This is the business end, what she's come for.

'Well, let's take it for granted that Spags Belgiovani and you,' she nods at Shorty, 'know how to grow marijuana, but can you tell me how you are going to get it to your customers?'

'Bikie gangs. Mine and Killer's,' Animal shouts, dead chuffed he can make a contribution at last. 'We's got chapters, brothers all over the fu . . . the country.'

'That's transport, not distribution,' Wendy replies.

I can't believe me ears. Where does she get this stuff from, she a bloody school teacher when she isn't running a greasy spoon?

Animal looks confused and Killer Kowolski next to him shrugs his shoulders, 'A deal is thirty bucks. It ain't hard, lady. We'll work the pubs, if it's okay by you?'

'Fair enough,' I think.

'Killer, how much do you think a bone-marrow transplant costs?' Wendy asks him.

'I wouldn't have a clue, lady,' Killer says. Killer likes his women to know their place, which is basically on the pillion seat of his Harley.

'Twenty thousand dollars. That's an estimate and if we can find a donor.' She reaches for her handbag and takes out a calculator and punches the buttons. After a few moments she looks up. 'At thirty dollars a bag that's 666 deals, the Devil's number. That just takes care of Anna, now what about the other kids who need help?' She looks at Killer, 'How long is it going to take you and Animal to sell that many deals through the nation's pubs?'

'Not just us, lady, the brothers, we've got a movement nationwide!' It's Animal again.

'Oh, the selling and distribution is to go outside this inner circle, the Dirty Dozen? Everybody and his dog Spot is going to be a dope merchant for the cause, are they?'

I'm looking down at me boots. 'Shit, Wendy, leave off, will ya?' I'm saying to meself. Now she's embarrassing the bejesus out of two of me brothers. Killer ain't gunna like it one bit. Like Animal, he likes his birds with big tits and zipped lips. Animal's probably never even spoken to a bird with his trousers on.

There is sudden silence. Like you can hear a pin drop. Then Lawsy laughs from the back. 'Okay, fair enough, Wendy. But if Griffith is a small town, what would you call Currawong Creek? As I understand it you were born and raised here? How are you, or we, for that matter, going to do it differently? What do you know about the civilian jungle, Sydney, Melbourne, Brisbane and the rest of the urban sprawls?'

'When Thommo was in Vietnam, that was before we were married, I spent four years in Sydney,' Wendy replies. I think she's glad to get away from cross-examining Killer and Animal. 'I couldn't find a job as a teacher, as city vacancies were impossible to get, so I joined a small advertising agency and also worked in a supper club at night for a couple of years until my salary in the ad agency increased. My folk needed the money to pay off the mortgage on Smoky Joe's and the job paid pretty well.' She flicks her hair back and grins, 'I've got a fair idea of the urban jungle. As a matter of fact, I've been propositioned by the best and the worst and survived both.' She looks around the room and then at me, 'In case you're thinking anything, gentlemen, Mr Thompson married a virgin when he returned to make what's laughingly known as his attempt at civilian life.'

The boys all laugh at this crack at me. But they've all got this guilty look on their gobs, I know they're thinking that maybe Wendy was like hinting that she was on 'the game' in Sydney.

Lawsy stands up and we all turn to look at him, 'I vote we start the serious meeting,' he says. 'We haven't a collective clue how we are going to go about this thing. But one thing I do know, what we don't need is a quarrel. Wendy's raised a few points and has shown she can put a thought or two together on her own. She's got under our skin a fair bit, but that's not necessarily a bad thing. And, I take her point, she is a Vietnam veteran.' He stops talking and looks around, 'What say we include Mrs Thompson, er . . . beg your pardon, Wendy, in?'

There is a moment's silence and then a bit of a laugh and then a bit of clapping. I look around and everyone seems happy except for Animal and Killer Kowolski, who are crouched forward, elbows on their knees, looking down at their boots.

Shorty picks this up at the same time as me, 'Killer? Animal? What do you reckon?'

Killer Kowolski looks up slowly, 'Mate, I dunno. I just dunno. I don't like it.'

'Me too,' Animal grunts, glad Killer's said it first.

'Well, it's got to be one in, all in,' Shorty says, 'We're not splitting the platoon.'

I glance over at Wendy, who is also looking down at her boots. Poor little bugger is still standing and now she looks alone, isolated, confused like.

'If I could make a proposal?' I say and stand up.

Shorty nods and I turn to face the boys. 'Let's listen to what Mrs Thompson has to say,' I say, real formal, 'Then, if at the end of the meeting we think she can't make a contribution, or can't work with us, we tell her?'

Wendy's head shoots up, 'No, that's the very purpose of *this* meeting, that's why you brought me here. Sorry, but no!' She turns to Shorty, 'I agree, the decision has to be unanimous.'

Well, I reckon that little outburst will just about see us two out of the room and headed for home with me packin' me bags for keeps.

Then Macca speaks up slow and quiet. 'You know, if Wendy were one of us and she'd come up with the exact selfsame arguments as she has today, I reckon we'd be pretty impressed. We'd be saying to ourselves that at least one of us is thinking straight. So why ain't we saying that now?'

'Most of us are,' Lawsy calls out.

'Okay, no point in going on like this, we'll put it to the vote,' Shorty says. 'But before we do I've got something to say. Relax, it may take a few minutes.' He clears his throat and begins.

'Six months ago I drove up from the farm to see Thommo, to ask him to come to a reunion dinner in Griffith. I could have called him on the phone I expect, but it seemed like a good excuse to have a couple of beers with a mate. The dinner was just gunna be us four locals, Lawsy and Spags, him and me, a tinnie or two and bit of a chin-wag about old times.

'Well, I get to the cafe and Thommo's out somewhere and I get to talk to Wendy, who I haven't seen since her and Thommo's wedding. One thing leads to another and she tells me about her little girl Anna. How she's got cancer of the blood. I ask the question, "Can it be cured?"

'It's very doubtful, she tells me. Finding a donor that's suitable for a bone-marrow transplant isn't easy. Even if they did, the operation would cost twenty grand. She doesn't go on about it and we then talk about Agent Orange, all the usual stuff, what it's doing to veterans' children and how the government is denying everything and taking no responsibility.

'Thommo doesn't turn up so I leave and tell Wendy if he gets in I'm having a beer at the pub if he wants to join me. I'm having a quiet ale on my own when this kid walks in. He's about eighteen, got the knees out of his jeans, his hair is damn near down to his waist and the whole of him looks like he could use a bloody good scrub. He goes over to the Kiwi barmaid and asks if she knows how to contact Peter Thompson?

'"Yeah," she says, and points, "Out the door to your left, Smoky Joe's Cafe, just down the road."

'He thanks her and turns to go. "He ain't there," I call out. Then on a hunch I say, "But he told me to expect you."

'The hippie kid props and takes a look at me, "I don't think so," he says. He's seen me short back 'n' sides and I can tell he's thinking it's the fuzz and that he's being set up for a bust. He looks at the door, but thinks better of it. If I'm inside, then there's someone waiting outside to grab him. He's a pretty cool customer. "Thanks for the offer, sir," he says real polite, "I was told I must only see Mr Thompson." He smiles, "No offence, hey? It's like, you know, personal business."

'I've already figured he's selling dope, or pills. "Righto, son, suit yerself, if you stick around, Mr Thompson may be coming along later," I turn back to my beer. Then out of the corner of my eye I see him go to the toilet. I wait a moment then follow him in. He's halfway through the window above the urinal when I jerk him down by the legs and he falls back into the porcelain in amongst the camphor tablets.' Shorty grins, 'I'm sorely tempted to pull the chain, a wash would have done him good. I pull him to his feet and maintain a fairly firm grip to the back of his neck, "Righto, hand it over, everything!" I hold out my free hand. He doesn't protest and he hands me over three little plastic bags of dope. "The money?" He takes out a stash and puts it into my hand, it looks like fives and tens mostly. "How much here?"

'"Three hundred dollars," he says.

'"Been a good day, eh?"

'"Until now," he replies.

'I laugh, "Well, kid, this is your lucky day." I hand him back the money and two of the three plastic bags. Then I hold up the other one. "How much?"

'"Thirty bucks, but you can have it for free if you don't take me in, sir." I let go his neck and give him thirty bucks, thinking I'll keep the dope for Thommo if he comes in. Then I stand aside and nod in the direction of the toilet door, "Garn, scarper! Hey, don't sell that shit to schoolkids!" I shout after him. Scrawny little bastard can't believe his luck and he's off like a rat up a drainpipe.

'Well, I look at this little plastic bag and think about how much of the stuff I could grow on a couple of acres. Then, out of the blue, the idea of growing dope and getting us all together like this to help veterans' sick kids comes to me.

'As you all know, I'm not the world's most impulsive bloke, so I sit and stew on it a while and try to think the whole thing out. A couple of weeks go by and I decide to call Wendy, find out more about the kid, you know, hospital costs and all that. She tells me and, of course, wants to know why I'm asking. Well, what the hell, she won't dob me in if Thommo's in the habit of smoking funny cigarettes, so I tell her confidentially what I'm thinking.'

Shorty glances over at Wendy, 'I don't think she was all that impressed. She don't say nothing for a while, then she says, "Can I think about it?" Well, I take that to mean she don't like the idea. Which is okay, she's a civilian, what can you expect, if the scam works I'll find a way to help them anyway.

'Then she calls me a week later and asks if we can meet. She'll drive to Griffith and meet me there. We meet at Griffith and she tells me she wants to know more.

'"Have you spoken to Thommo?" I say. She says she hasn't. "Why not?" I ask.

'"Because I don't want him to get his hopes up," she says. Then she tells me she likes the plan but it's against the law.

'"It's Agent Orange that's done this to your girlie,

144

ain't it?" I argue back. "If the government won't do anything, we're forced to take the law in our own hands."

'"That can't be proved, Shorty. Lots of children die of leukaemia and they're not all vets' kids. It may not be Agent Orange in Anna's case."

'"Yeah, well, we can still raise the money for you. Twenty grand, that's not impossible. It doesn't matter how it happened, besides there's lots of other bad things happening – cleft palate, cleft lip, spina bifida, gross deformities, strange things happening to vets' children that don't happen anything like as frequently in the general population. The only thing these children have in common is their daddy served in Vietnam."

'Then she comes out and says, "Shorty, it's not the twenty thousand dollars it will cost for the operation. If it was we'd happily sell Smoky Joe's to pay to get Anna better. The problem is finding the right donor. Our best chance is a relative and Thommo and me have no family to speak of. The thing is, we could test a million potential donors and not come up with a suitable one."

'Well, that kind of puts the kybosh on things. There's not a whole lot I could say after that,' Shorty says.

'"But it's still a good idea and I'd like to be a part of it," Wendy then says to me. "There are lots of other children in trouble. Vietnamese children as well as ours, they're all just sick kids who need help."

'I shake my head, "No way, Wendy. We could all go to gaol if the scam doesn't work. If I can get the platoon who fought at Long Tan together, they may buy the plan. I figure most of the blokes will reckon they ain't got a helluva lot to lose anyway. But there's no way they're gunna buy it with someone from the outside involved. I mean no offence, love, but someone who ain't a Vietnam veteran, least of all a woman with a small, sick child, would not be welcome."

'Wendy then gives me the routine you just heard, how she's also a Vietnam veteran. I shake my head, "I can't see it happening. No way!" Then she comes back again, "So I'm happy to put my husband in danger, that's okay, is it?" I tell her that's up to him, nobody's going to force him.'

Shorty looks around the room and then directly at me. He can see I'm totally gobsmacked, but he pretends not to notice. 'Well, as you've seen, Mrs Thompson doesn't take no for an answer. This morning Thommo came to me and put the hard word on me and I decide we'll have this meeting and let the brothers decide.'

Shorty shrugs and then he goes on, 'What I'm trying to say now is Wendy knows her little daughter isn't gunna benefit from anything we do, but, as you can see, she still wants to help. She knows the risks she's taking. Well, there yer go then. It's over to you, gentlemen. Let's vote on it. But it's all in or none and no more discussion.'

I'm too scared to look, besides, I can't believe what I've just heard. Jesus H. Christ! But I raise my hand anyway and I fix my eyes on Wendy, who doesn't look at me. There's a chorus of Ayes. Then I see her smile. 'Thank you, gentlemen,' she says quietly, 'I won't let you down.'

I don't know whether to go over and belt her or kiss her, but one thing I know for sure, she wasn't never gunna dump me, wasn't gunna give me my marching orders. It was all a ploy. I'm learning stuff about my wife I don't know.

The boys get up for a break before the next meeting starts with a new forward scout elected to the platoon they could never have imagined. I've still got me doubts about the whole thing and I wonder if me wife's got the peripheral vision she's gunna need in the civilian jungle?

Maybe, maybe not, but she's already got one good qualification for jungle warfare, she don't wear underpants.

Chapter Five

Shorty has done his homework. What he doesn't know about growing marijuana ain't worth knowing. Or so it seems to us. He doesn't say where he gets his info, instead he gives us this long, boring lecture. Later we find out it's from Nam Tran.

In fairness, his briefing probably isn't that long, but the hangovers are beginning to lift and, as every warrior knows, the best way to hasten this process is to build the beginnings of another one.

I don't know why Wendy needs to know all this stuff, Shorty and Spags can take care of the growing department and the rest of us can do as we're told, same as the army. Shorty is enjoying himself, doing the long-winded, and Wendy's questions are stirring the breeze he is causing to gale force. The sergeant and the school mistress, it's gunna turn out to be a bloody nightmare combination.

Soon enough the blokes are clasping their elbows and leaning on their knees, looking down at the space between their legs and giving out more than the occasional sigh.

Shorty goes on about climate, planting just before the spring rains, soil conditions, irrigation, plant quality, the use of nitrates, lime and spraying insecticides. Humans are not the only ones to like dope neither. It seems bugs go ape over marijuana and bug control is a big problem as every manner of insect likes to take a chomp of it. I've never ever thought about a snail being stoned but there you go, there's a lot of wicked stuff going on in mother nature we just don't know about.

Then Bongface mentions that there's different sorts of cannabis for the use of.

Wendy jumps on this. 'Different how?'

'Well, there's the heads that you roll into a joint and smoke, then there's hash and hash oil,' Bongface says.

'What's the difference?' she immediately wants to know.

'Some's better than others,' he says.

'Better how?' she asks.

'Yeah, well, good hash gets you stoned quicker and hash oil is supposed to be even faster and better.'

'Supposed? What's that mean?'

'Well, yeah, I ain't used hash oil.'

Nam Tran chips in, 'Hash oil very good, better, hash honey.'

'Hash honey? That's a lovely name,' Wendy says. 'It's the best, is it?'

'Very good, very expensive, to make this one very hard.'

'Can you make hash honey, Nam Tran?'

He nods, 'I can make.'

'And the price? On the market?'

Nam Tran shrugs. 'Hash honey, you not find Australia. China, Hong Kong, New York maybe, only rich man, also movie star have this.'

'And you can make it?' Wendy's eyes are shining.

Nam Tran turns his palms upwards, 'Of course.'

'What does hash honey do that the other dope doesn't?'

Nam Tran giggles and covers his mouth with his hand, 'I not say to a lady,' he says.

'Ah, it's an aphrodisiac, is it?'

'Excuse me?' the little man says, looking confused.

'Gives extra good sex,' Lawsy offers.

Nam Tran giggles again, 'Special one, many, many for women, for man, long, long time.'

We all laugh. I say to Wendy, 'Can't wait to try this hash honey, honey.'

'Thommo!' she exclaims. She's smiling, but I know that particular smile, it's strictly for public consumption. 'You'll keep,' she says and this brings another laugh. Wendy's winning the battle of the sexes and I can see the boys are getting to like her. They'd like her a lot better if only she'd stop asking so many goddamn questions and we could all go downstairs to the bar.

But she ain't finished yet. Nam Tran's English is pretty good but he has some trouble with getting her answers about this hash honey gear. Though after a while what comes out is that you use the stuff for just about anything. Mix it with butter and spread it on your toast, mix it into a drink, cover a pin with it and stick it down the front of a cigarette, spread it on a cigarette paper and use it with weed, bong it, hot knife it, you name it, this hash honey is the original convenience dope. What's more, whatever you do with it, it gives you a better, quicker and longer high. There's only one thing against it, it takes four times as much weed to make hash honey, which means it's gunna be very expensive on the street.

'Hah, that's wonderful, that's just what we need to know, thank you,' Wendy says at last. I tell you what, I'm beginning to wonder what sort of girl I've married.

The meeting goes on a while longer and arrangements are made for us to work with Shorty and Spags. You know, plough the land, get the crop planted.

It is decided that Nam Tran is going to set up a small laboratory to extract the oil and it will be located underground, Viet Cong style.

Shorty points to me, 'Thommo, you've worked as a builder's labourer and know a bit about construction, don't ya?'

'Sure, a bit,' I reply.

'Can you drive a back hoe, mix cement, lay a line o' bricks and do a bit o' plumbing?'

'Yep, three o' them things, I can't do electrical.' I think a moment. 'Don't expect too much, mate, it'll be about the same standard as my cooking.' Which brings a laugh.

'Electrician, that's your trade, ain't it, Flow?' Shorty asks.

'Yeah, no problems,' Flow answers.

'That'll do. Thommo, you're elected to be Nam Tran's offsider when he builds the lab, Flow will do the electrics when the time comes.'

Shorty and Spags are absorbing the cost of ploughing, fertiliser and pesticide and the cost of feeding us for the duration. They agree to be paid back later from our profits. In the pesticide area we make a resolution to use nothing that's harmful to humans, it's the least we can do seeing how this whole scam has become necessary.

Lawsy is the treasurer and accountant. The rest of us will give our time and Wendy is in charge of distribution and selling.

So, when you look at it, the most reliable are in the box seat, with the shit-kickers like me doing the labouring. It ain't all that different from the army.

The boys who come up originally from Sydney and elsewhere backtrack home for a few days to get their gear and tell their wives and girlfriends they'll be away for a month or so, no questions asked or explanations given to stickybeaks.

Most of the vets in our platoon have a habit of 'going bush', disappearing from time to time, so their women aren't that curious and, besides, they'll probably enjoy the break from a Vietnam vet.

Nam Tran, it seems, has been staying at Shorty's place all along. I move in the next day and help him fix up the citrus shed as a bunk house and lay a slab of cement and put in an open-air shower block and a bit of a kitchen for when the boys arrive back. Flow fixes the new electrical requirements when he gets up with the rest.

Ten days after the meeting at Smoky Joe's we are all assembled at Shorty's farm and ready for the kick-off.

We soon enough find out we've grown soft and the first few nights in the shed are really crook. But after a couple of days' work we're that buggered, we can sleep on a fencing rail with a roll of barbed wire for a pillow. Anyway, we keep comforting ourselves, it's a bloody sight better than kipping in a shell scrape under a hutchie during the monsoon season.

Me and Nam Tran done the cooking as well as working on the laboratory. The blokes come to refer to any given working day as a 'Grunt chow' day or a 'Nog chow' day. Grunt chow being bad and Nog chow good. They soon realise that after frying a bit of meat on the barbie, chopping up a few pounds of spuds and boiling up a bucketful of veggies or pasta my culinary ability is exhausted.

After a few days of my chow they go on strike and I'm put on breakfast duty frying eggs and bacon, my Smoky Joe's job as well as making the sangos for lunch. At night Nam Tran cooks and I prepare the veggies and stuff. Nam Tran cooks Chinese style with only one big cleaver as his cutting instrument and he wants me to do the same. It's got something to do with how you cut them or something. So I agree and I get to like using it and, after a while, I get pretty cocky. Chop, chop, chop in a blur, carrots, celery, onions diced and sliced before your very eyes. So one night the inevitable happens and the bloody thing damn near cuts my finger off.

'Shit!' I yell and Nam Tran comes running. 'I've cut me bloody finger off,' I scream.

Nam Tran grabs my hand and smothers it in a dish towel then he applies a tourniquet. 'Thommo, okay. Tran fix, short time, no worries.' He's perfectly calm like nothing much has happened and he makes me hold my arm above me head and pisses off only to arrive back a few minutes later with one o' them old-fashioned doctors' bags wharfies and labourers used to use. He opens it up and takes out gear and cleans and dresses the finger and then to my amazement starts to sew it together. It hurts like hell but he grins and I grin and wince a bit, but there's no doubt about it, he knows his onions. He stitches me up neat as you like and then bandages me like an expert. I've known MOs couldn't have done half as good a job.

Later I say to him, 'Hey, Nam Tran, where'd you learn to, yer know,' I hold up me bandaged finger, 'learn to do this stuff?'

He's frying rice and he looks up, 'North Vietnam Army.'

'Yeah? You saying all Nogs can do this?'

He laughs. 'No, special one, barefoot doctor.'

'Barefoot doctor?'

'Not many doctor in North Vietnam so we make some soldier barefoot doctor,' he explains further.

'What's that mean exactly, they go around without boots on?'

He shakes his head, 'Not doctor for studying in school to know everything medicine, only for wound. Battle wounds, this one barefoot doctor,' he adds by way of an explanation.

I nod, 'Oh yeah, I see. Well, you could've fooled me, mate. You did a bloody good job. I've seen a few sutures in me time, you're a flamin' expert.'

He points to the cleaver. 'Not same as you,' he says laughing. I can see he likes what I've said about the job he's done on me.

Anyway, over the next couple of weeks he tends to the finger real well and then takes out the stitches just as expert as he put them in. Tell you what, if all them barefoot doctors are as good as him I'd trust them any day over your average Oz army MO. Reckon the little bloke could whip your appendix out, no problems.

As we work together to build the underground laboratory I soon grow to admire the little Nog. The laboratory is situated beneath a huge old winemaking and packing shed fifty yards back of Shorty's house. Shorty's built a new shed closer to his grapevines and citrus orchards.

Nam Tran goes like a steam engine from dawn to dusk, but he don't get in the way or try to impress. I soon learn there's not much he don't know about underground construction. What's more, he's always got a smile on his gob as he shows me what to do so there's no way I can take offence.

Me and Nam Tran become real good mates. He can stand under me armpit with room to spare but he's true blue and a man has to run to keep up with him. By the end of the day I'm whacked and he's into making the dinner, still smiling.

The entrance to the laboratory is concealed inside one of these old wine barrels. There's also a big old vat with a chimney going through the roof and Nam Tran turns this into the main ventilation shaft, lining it with pink fibre-glass bats to kill the noise. Ventilation is not only necessary for breathing but it turns out to be critical for the making of hash honey, which uses a lot of butane gas.

From the outside nothing looks changed, just an old wine distillery and packing shed with this broken-down, dusty equipment in it. There's still electricity in the shed and it's a simple matter for Flow to wire the lab for lights and to put in an exhaust fan and the other gear Nam Tran needs. You could walk into the shed and be standing right on top of the laboratory and even with the exhaust fan blowing you wouldn't hear a thing. No wonder the Nogs were so hard to beat.

I must say, it's amazing what we've built underground to Nam Tran's instructions. There's a complete facility for making large quantities of hash oil. Him and me have also put a ceiling in the old wine shed using very old floorboards. Nam Tran's even built a bit of a buckle into it so it looks like it's been there for yonks and is about to fall down. Inside the roof are the drying facilities for the harvested weed and he's also got a ventilation system that makes sure the crop is cured slow and perfect at around 21°C.

Once the crop is harvested, the idea is to dry it and reduce it to the raw material required to turn it into hash honey as quick as possible for storage underground. Except for the lab, there is to be nothing on the surface to hide. Shorty takes one more precaution, only a couple of us will know the exact location of the laboratory.

I mean we all know there is a laboratory on the

property but the rest think it's underground somewhere among the brigalow scrub. The citrus packing shed where we sleep and cook is a good mile and a half away from the main house and Weed Valley, as the planting location is called, is half a mile still further out so they don't observe Nam Tran and my movements during the day.

'What they don't know can't hurt us,' Shorty says to me one day.

'Mate, I'm not happy keeping stuff back from the mob. You said it yerself, one in all in,' I protest.

'Thommo, like the army, we're all fighting the same war, but some of us know more than others. It's been a while since Vietnam. Things change, some of our blokes are under a lot of psychological pressure, and in the hands of a big hairy-arsed cop anything could happen. We might be okay when we're together, trust each other with our lives. But alone and under stress people have been known to talk, even when they think they're not. When we harvest the weed I want there to be no trace of it left. If only you, Nam Tran, and me know the exact location of the lab and the drying shed, I'm going to sleep a whole lot better at night.'

'What about Flow?'

He'd forgotten about Flow. 'Yeah,' he now says, knowing what I mean. 'I'll have a talk to him.'

Afterwards, when I think about it, and I should've before, I'm that ashamed of myself. A man's a fool to think any different to Shorty. He's the fall guy in all this. If the crop or the lab gets discovered on his property, he's the bloke who gets the five years in the clink and a fine that would damn near bankrupt him. He has every right to be a tad cautious even with the brothers.

The plan is, that the moment the crop is harvested the plants are to be uprooted and burned, with not a stem remaining. Weed Valley will then be sown with winter oats, clean as a whistle for anyone to see. But the lab and the drying shed will still be on the property for months afterwards.

It turns out Nam Tran has been setting up a seedling nursery for about three months. When we get there he has nearly a thousand healthy marijuana seedlings ready for planting out.

I can't help wondering what Shorty would have done if we'd turned down the idea. I mean, would you burn a fortune's worth of healthy marijuana seedlings? He must have been pretty confident that we'd go along with the scam. Better not think about that one too much, hey?

Sharing accommodation and working all day together isn't all sunshine and happy smiles. As one of the platoon section commanders and the biggest bloke among us, I'm sort of elected the peacemaker in the group. This takes up a fair bit of my time as getting along with others don't come natural to most of us any longer.

Planting out seedlings is back-breaking work and if one of the boys is malingering the others get cranky as hell. They forget we all have our off days. Also, being told what to do don't go down too well neither. Most nights it's something that one of the boys has said to another and which has been took the wrong way and caused a bit of aggro that needs sorting.

Privately we all dread the nights. That's when we can get out of control. With no grog or dope to calm the nerves each of us is secretly scared of the nightmares that we know sooner or later must surely come.

But we're so physically clapped out that sleep becomes a necessity and, as a mob, we seem to be generally less spooked than usual. I know I am.

Gazza, though, has two real crook nights during the month and both times we have to pour a bucket o' cold water over him to bring him out of his half-awake berserk state o' mind. It's bloody scary seeing it happen with someone else and knowing you've done the same yourself. I now see what Wendy's been through and I'm ashamed of meself. Most nights one or another of the boys wakes us up screaming out and thrashing around, trying to escape their sleeping bag.

Knives and clubs, the very things that give us the confidence to go to sleep, have to be stashed so that there won't be any serious accidents. It's my job to go around last thing to kick at every sleeping bag, see that no one has a four b' two he's placed inside it in case they get spooked in their dreams and half wake up and go on the attack. It took six of us to hold Gazza down, even without a weapon.

The point is, we've all been there before, so an incident during the night don't get talked about or a fuss made. It's almost like being back together in the jungle. You know somehow, even in your nightmare, that your buddies are there with you and they're not going to desert you in a crisis. Maybe I just invented that, but I know I was better in the citrus shed than at home.

We get through the ploughing and planting and setting up the irrigation pumps and piping and fencing the area. After a month or so of hard yakka we're fitter than we've been in quite a while and a few of the bellies around are considerably flattened, mine included.

The crop is planted and the spring rains come on

time and we're feeling pretty damned pleased with ourselves with all the little dope plants standing up straight in long rows, like they're on parade.

Shorty draws up a roster system where each of us will come back for a period of two weeks during the growing season, two blokes at a time. Our job is to guard and tend the crop until harvest time. We throw a bit of a party where we all get pissed for the first time in a month before the rest of us go back home.

The easy part is over. Detection is now the big worry, though the crop is in a secluded little valley which you can only approach through a dense stand of brigalow and then a six-foot-high fence. Shorty assures us it's hard to see from the air, though anyone flying low over it ain't gunna mistake what's growing down there for next season's rice crop.

We've got one thing good going for us, marijuana isn't really being grown on a commercial scale in Australia yet. Or if it is, there's never been a major bust. Mostly it's hippie communes growing small batches in the bush for their own use and as a bit of a cash or trade crop on the side. The fuzz won't be out looking at the daily doings of your basic farmer, nor will they ever suspect it is to be grown in a big way in the middle of the rice-rich Riverina.

Almost all the weed and hash sold in Australia is still imported from Asia. The cops and various State drug squads are mostly into making busts on the street, in airports and at the docks.

We've got six months before we harvest and then sell our product and so every Wednesday arvo the two warriors on roster and the six locals, Shorty, Spags, Lawsy, Nam Tran, Wendy and me, have a meeting at Smoky Joe's to discuss the operation. In this way everyone is eventually updated and briefed.

It is over this period that Wendy comes into her own. She's the forward scout and it's her responsibility, with Lawsy, to organise the selling and legal-protection arm of the operation. I dunno how she fits it in, I don't get back to help in the cafe for the first two months and she has to run it alone except for the weekends when I get home.

Unfortunately little Anna is back at the Children's Hospital for another bout of chemotherapy and so weekends Wendy flies down to Sydney and back to see her. She gets other stuff done while she's there, but when I ask her about this she laughs, then says, 'Secret women's business, Thommo.' She's working her butt off and I've never seen her better, she seems to be thriving on the challenge she's been given.

One evening I'm standing with Shorty at the edge of

Weed Valley, the plants are now about three feet high. 'It's like looking at a vault full of money,' I say, then I point to a weed plant near me, 'Every one of them little buggers are worth a fortune.'

'Only 50 per cent of them,' Shorty says.

'How come?' I ask.

'Half of those plants are male, and when they come into bud we're going to have to weed them out.'

'Shit, hey? You can't tell the sex when they're seedlings?'

I shouldn't have asked. Shorty goes into this technical explanation which I won't repeat. But it seems there are male and female marijuana plants and the males must be gotten rid of before pollination.

The crop comes along a treat and, apart from the insects which are always having a go at it and keeping the weeds down, it's not hard to look after. This is how you can tell they're male, the buds have these little balls that hang off a bit of a stem and they don't have these little white hairs coming out of them like the female buds.

The female buds are called sinsemilla. I don't suppose you need to know this, but with the male pollen missing, the females use all their energy to grow thick with unfertilised flowers. In a few more weeks these unfertilised flowers are the real McCoy, they produce the resin called THC, the stuff that dreams are made of.

It's a shit of a job getting the male plants out, you have to be real careful not to shake the plant in case some early female buds open and you cause fertilisation.

Harvesting comes at last and the boys begin arriving. Shorty and Spags pick them up in Griffith at night and bring them in. For several days Nam Tran has been going around smelling the crop and one morning I go with him.

'You smell, Thommo,' he says and points to a flower. I take a sniff and it smells sort of musky sweet. Then he shows me the resin that has formed on each of the tiny buds that have turned from white to amber. 'Tomorrow okay,' he says, grinning at me, then he waves his arm to indicate the whole of Weed Valley. 'Special this one, very, very good for oil.'

We work at dusk and into the night using torches. This is not to conceal our activities, but the best time to harvest is after sundown. In nine nights we've cut the stems holding the mature heads and carefully transported them to a waiting truck. I drive the truck to the wine shed and Nam Tran, Shorty and myself hang the stems for drying in the ceiling.

There's over ten tons of good heads and we can't

believe we've got away with it. Nam Tran and Shorty calculate there's potentially three million bucks' worth of hash oil at current retail prices. If we convert the oil into hash honey, Christ alone knows what it will be worth.

Lawsy gives us a talk about being 'caught in possession'. Suddenly it becomes very real to us all that we're not just playing a game, we are back in the jungle, only this time we're the bad guys.

'Okay, let me give you a few facts,' Lawsy begins. 'In the past few months I've been keeping a watch on drug convictions and there's one or two things you ought to know,' Lawsy begins. 'The first and most important is, tell the police your name and address and nothing more. Understand? Nothing! Bugger all else.

'If they come with a warrant, don't let them into your house until you've read it very carefully and very slowly, so you can get your wits together and hopefully your wife or girlfriend is busy out the back flushing the toilet for disposal. Get the idea?'

We all nod and he continues, 'Just remember, 98 per cent of people charged with possession are convicted on their own statement. Shut yer gob. Name and address, nothing else. If you are arrested, you must accompany the cops to the police station. If you are not under arrest, don't volunteer to accompany them or agree if they ask you to do so for the sake of cooperating.

'The police have only one objective, to get a conviction, and they'll do that a damn sight better when you're on their territory.

'Now, if they get you to the cop station and they're interrogating you, no matter what they do, give you a backhand, threaten you, use heated language, insult you, your mother or your wife, make you accidentally on purpose fall off a chair and injure yourself, just cop it sweet. A few bruises are better than twelve months in the clink. Just keep repeating, "I have nothing to say, I wish to see my lawyer."

'Now, there's something else, there's other means of getting stuff out of you. They may ask questions that seem real innocent, like, "Where do your parents live?" Well, you can't see much harm in answering so you tell them. Now you have answered a direct question and if you refuse to answer other directly related questions, this means you are answering selectively and the judge is likely to frown upon this and you may cop a sentence or a fine.'

Lawsy shoots out his arm, pointing at us, 'Now, remember, boys, you are *only* exercising your right to say *nothing*.

'Okay, one last thing. If there's two of you caught, the cops will separate you, sooner or later a cop will come into the room and whisper to the fuzz who are drilling you. They will then look elated and tell you your mate has confessed, that he or she has come clean. Ignore this, even if they tell you they now have enough evidence without your cooperation to prosecute. Whatever evidence they've got, you can't make things worse for yourself by remaining silent, keeping your trap shut.'

Shorty then talks to us about never giving away the location of the farm, not even to our wives or girlfriends, and he says Wendy is going to brief us on what he calls 'Operation Civilian Jungle' or OCJ.

Wendy is dressed like she was the day we accepted her as our forward scout, it's the boots and the skintight jeans but because it's like well into summer she's wearing a pale pink shirt with the top four buttons not being put to work, so that the rise and fall of her breathing is very bloody apparent. Her hair is like a halo around her head and she's so pretty I want to cry, but I also want to do up them buttons.

I'm also scared. Suddenly it's all gunna happen and my little darling is the boss of the dangerous part. Old Thommo is out of his depth, the person I love the most in the world is now beyond my protection. She's the general and I'm the grunt. I can tell ya, it don't feel good and I can't help thinking, 'Shit, there's nothing in it for us, for Anna, why are we doing this?'

Chapter Six

It's time to take a bit of a leap forward. Nam Tran's hash honey is about as good as hash can get, super-refined oil four times stronger than any other form of weed. Wendy has a plan for getting it out to the public that works pretty well from day one, though at first we think she's crazy. She calls it 'infiltration into the market'.

'In any market,' she explains, 'you've got to get your first users, the early adopters of your product, they lead the way for others.'

'What's wrong with just flogging it down the pub?' Killer wants to know. 'Blokes there will try anything once.'

'Too expensive, hash honey isn't for your regular pub crowd. We've got to make it fashionable, the drug of choice with the beautiful people, where the fact that it's very expensive adds to its appeal. If we can do this, then we achieve several things.'

'Like what?' Flow Murray asks.

'Well, firstly, we keep it away from school children. It's too expensive and the method of distribution prevents them obtaining it. Secondly, the cops are not going to be all that interested in a designer drug that doesn't add to the crime statistics, nobody is going to mug a citizen or rob a house to pay for it.'

'What about being found in possession?' Lawsy asks. Even though he knows the answer, he wants us all to hear it from Wendy.

'What cop is going to bust a well-known socialite or a big-time businessman? It's not the sort of crime-busting headline they're looking for. What's more, hash honey is not something your average policeman knows about. You can easily recognise weed and if it's being used when they make a bust you can smell it. Hash honey isn't like that.

'On the other hand,' Wendy adds, 'if we're caught flogging it, as Lawsy explained, that's another matter. Dealing is definitely different, but then you all know the drill, the way we've set things up. If you follow procedure and never deviate you're unlikely to be caught dealing.'

I'm amazed at all this. I knew Wendy worked in an advertising agency but she's never talked about this kind of thing to me before. I guess the problems with Anna sort of took care of what was on her mind. There's no doubt Wendy's done her homework and this is what she's done.

On her weekends in Sydney she stays with Mo's sister, Maureen, who is a hairdresser. Not your run-of-the-mill hairdresser, you understand, but one of your multiple-award-winning triple-certificate hairdressers who cuts and styles in an upmarket salon in Double Bay called Le Gaye at the Bay.

The salon is owned by a bloke called Trenton le Gaye, who, when you come to think about it, has a pretty handy name for a poofter who's also a hairdresser. In fact, it turns out his name was invented for the very purpose. Maureen says his real name is Wayne Sprogg, which is not a moniker you'd want to wear if you're going to be a darling of the Sydney social set.

Trenton claims to have trained in London and then worked in LA, where, it is said, he did Audrey Hepburn's hair for *Breakfast at Tiffany's*, even though that was shot in New York. In fact, Maureen says he was the number-eight hairdresser on the set and only once briefly touched her hair with a brush between takes.

He come back to Sydney because his lover got the job of running the Australian branch of a US parcel dispatch company.

Trenton le Gaye styles all the models for *Vogue* magazine and just about all the beautiful people in town, which, of course, also includes all of the ugly people, the rule being that as long as they will pay sixty bucks for a haircut and they regularly get their mugs in the social columns then they're dinky-di le Gaye material.

Maureen is Trenton's cutter supremo, he's nicknamed her 'Jacka the wonder hacker', and she is making real big bickies as his right-hand man. Which is not a misuse of the expression, because Mo's sister's a chick with a lot more balls than her boss.

Women go to le Gaye's to be seen and to have other women point to their hair at a cocktail party and say, 'Darling, your hair looks fabulous, is that a le Gaye?' In fact it's a le Maureen, but that's show biz for you. Le Gaye gets all the credit when all he does is ponce around the salon spreading and listening to goss.

Occasionally, if there's someone with a big rep in the salon, the darling of the Double Bay social set will grab the scissors from Maureen and do a bit of a token snip, though he's bloody careful not to screw up what she's already done. There you go, darling (snip, snip),

Maureen's a real wizard with the scissors (ha, ha), I'm just the sorcerer's apprentice (snip, snip), she's a national treasure (snip), shouldn't interfere (snip, snip), it's just that one loves so to meddle (snip), to keep one's humble little fingers flying.' (Stand back, cup chin with thumb and forefinger, look at client with head to one side, snip, snip, mostly air.) 'Ah, yes, God is in the details, divine, my dear, even if I say so myself. *Moi* hasn't lost his touch.'

The meddle adds ten bucks to the price of the cut and does bugger all except allows the client to legitimately claim that 'Himself' personally cut her hair. Afterwards Maureen takes the ten bucks he added to the bill out of the till as a tax-free bonus.

The other thing about this type of salon, probably every type of hairdresser, is that women tell hairdressers their deepest darkest secrets and dish the dirt as well as hear the latest gossip on everyone else. You know, who's sleeping with who, whose husband can't get it up. More importantly, whose old man has been seen dining in a little-known restaurant with someone twenty years younger than himself. Whose boyfriend isn't responding in bed. Who's available, who isn't. Who got drunk at a reception and disgraced themselves. Who just had a face-lift or the new liposuction to reduce their hips and bum and flatten their gut. All the good smut women like to feed into their conversations during long lunches in smart restaurants, at dinners and cocktail parties, or over the phone to their stickybeak mates.

If women are depressed when they come into Le Gaye at the Bay, they go away feeling a whole heap better, armed with a new hairdo, nails painted fire-engine red, eyelashes tinted and enough gossip to inflict severe damage to several top-banana reputations. It doesn't seem to occur to them that they've deposited as much potential smut about themselves for the use of, as they've taken away.

So Maureen tells Wendy all this in the process of her weekend visits to see Anna and soon enough Wendy's got the perfect infiltration marketing plan. She suggests that Maureen becomes a part of the Smoky Joe scam and that she introduces a new summer drink into the salon.

'What sort of drink?' Maureen asks. 'I mean, what goes well with this hash honey?'

'Just about anything,' Wendy replies.

'Have you made up a few drinks, tasted them?'

Wendy admits she hasn't. She's a bit afraid even though she knows it isn't addictive. With little Anna so sick she's scared she'll become psychologically addicted, you know, come to depend on the stuff.

'Hey, are you serious?' Maureen says. 'I'm supposed to make up a drink that's going to make people want to buy hash honey and you haven't even tried it?'

'Well, no, yes, I mean Thommo smokes the stuff, I thought I'd leave it at that?'

'Well, I'm not going to try it on my own! What's more, I'm not going to offer our clients something that may have the wrong effect on them.' She grins at Wendy, 'So let's start experimenting right now, girl.'

As Wendy later confesses she and Maureen had a couple of very interesting weekends experimenting. They decide to keep the drink simple, though it has to have an alcohol base to dissolve the hash honey as it is fat or alcohol soluble. They simply take a teaspoon of vodka, which is tasteless, and dissolve two drops of hash honey into it and then add lime juice, soda, a saccharine tablet to sweeten it, a slice of lemon and ice. In the winter it will simply be tea or coffee, the milk acting as the fat soluble, or if taken black, a teaspoon of vodka is added. The new drink has all the refreshment of the lime juice with a slightly bitter taste that survives the saccharine and makes it interesting. It's served in a smallish glass so that the client doesn't just take a couple of sips and leave the rest.

'What will I call it?' Maureen wants to know.

Wendy thinks for a while, then says, 'Nam Tran once told me the tiger is an important symbol for the Vietnamese people, why not call it Tiger Honey?'

Maureen laughs, 'Roughly translated that's tiger piss! What about White Tiger? I could sell that to our clients.' She continues, '"Madam, may I get you a White Tiger, it's our new summer refresher?"'

Most women come into the hairdressers a bit hassled or stressed and Maureen soon learns to pick her mark. Not everyone is right for a White Tiger, but those who are come in depressed and leave on a high, feeling great, what Maureen comes to call 'a light stone'. This means they can function perfectly but every sensation is heightened, colours seem brighter, problems seem easy to solve, people are nicer and work becomes a breeze and the buzz lasts five hours. What's more there are no hangovers.

Pretty soon customers coming in make a point of asking for a White Tiger. 'What is it? It can't simply be lime juice and soda?'

'Oh, we add secret herbs and spices,' Maureen says, smiling.

'Secret herbs? C'mon, you must know what it is?'

'No, I really don't,' Maureen fibs, 'I think it's something that's popular in Hong Kong, you know, a common drink.'

This usually brings a bit of a frightened look, 'It's not addictive, is it?'

Maureen, who has rehearsed all this with Wendy, laughs, 'No, it's something the Chinese have used for thousands of years, you know sort of like ginseng, a natural stimulant or relaxant, whatever your mood happens to be at the time.' Which, of course, is the absolute truth.

Then one day Wendy's big break comes. Maureen's styling the hair of a Magazine Queen named Dotty Marche, who's sipping on a White Tiger.

'Maureen, I've asked you about this drink before, where do you get the herbs you use in it? I'd like to buy some. Is that possible?'

Maureen doesn't answer for a moment, then she says quietly, 'I'm not sure I can help you, Dotty.'

Dotty is now dead curious and even a bit miffed. She's one of those sheilas used to getting her own way. 'And why? You said it wasn't illegal, so why not?'

'I said it wasn't addictive.'

'Well, that's the same thing, isn't it?'

Maureen looks all innocent like, 'Well, I don't know . . . I suppose?'

'In that case, just tell me where you buy the stuff?' Maureen, looking into the mirror, sees Dotty Marche's right eyebrow rise slightly. She's not going to be fobbed off.

Maureen appears to hesitate, 'It's this card, the one the bikie gave me, it's . . . well, it's a bit embarrassing.'

'Can I see it?' Dotty asks. 'It'll take a fair bit to embarrass me, my girl.'

'Well, it's like a registered customer card, you can't just buy the herb essence, you have to have your own number to order.'

'So it *is* illegal!' Dotty exclaims. 'How very interesting.'

'I really don't know,' Maureen insists, 'It's just how it's done.' By now Dotty is hooked, 'Get me the card, girl, let me see for myself.'

Maureen goes out the back and a few moments later comes back in and hands the woman a card. Dotty looks at it and bursts into laughter. She's holding Wendy's hash honey calling card. It's got this Chinese calligraphy on it which is the sign of the tiger and below it, it says:

虎

White Tiger
Keeps you coming and him going.
Phone: 555 1369

'So it wasn't my imagination!' Dotty says.

'Imagination?' Maureen asks, pretending to be surprised.

Then Dotty tells Maureen how she'd been so horny after the last White Tiger that she'd practically raped her partner. 'Poor darling didn't quite know what had hit him!'

'You're not the first to say that,' Maureen giggles. This is also part of what she and Wendy have rehearsed.

'Well, that's wonderful. Have you used it, you know, in this way yourself?' she now asks Maureen.

Maureen laughs, 'I'm not saying.'

Dotty Marche claps her hands, 'You have, haven't you?'

'It just helps you relax,' Maureen says, turning off the hairdryer.

'And I call this number? Can I write it down?' Dotty holds up the card.

'Sure, but first turn the card over, see what it says on the back.'

Dotty Marche flips the card and reads:

For your personal privacy
always call from a public phone.

Dotty grins, 'It *must* be illegal.' She reaches over and takes a small notebook from her bag and copies down the number. 'I haven't used a public phone in years, how exciting.'

'This herb essence, it isn't cheap,' Maureen says. 'Trenton thinks of it as a special treat for his best customers.'

'How much?'

'A week's supply, I mean if you were to make say two drinks a day, is a hundred dollars.'

Dotty sniffs and holds up the card again, 'Darling, if it does what it promises here, it will be an absolute bargain.'

'By the way,' Maureen then says, 'it comes in liquid form.' She explains how you can mix it.

'At last, the ultimate and positively sneaky aphrodisiac,' Dotty exclaims.

'Stimulant or relaxant, that's all it claims to be,' Maureen laughs.

Wendy's system is simple enough. When the prospect calls she is met with an answerphone which asks her to wait and automatically dials a second number where another recorded voice gives her the following message:

Thank you for calling. When you hear the beep you

will be given thirty seconds to nominate a precise time and location anywhere in the central business district of Sydney between the Town Hall and Circular Quay. You will be met there in three days. Look for a woman wearing a red rose. You will greet her by saying 'White Tiger' and she will reply by saying 'Smoky'. Bring a sealed envelope containing one hundred dollars. You now have thirty seconds.

So this is how a typical exchange is worked. Dotty Marche meets her Smoky and goes through the routine. The Smoky takes the envelope, doesn't open it and puts it in her bag, then she removes the rose and pins it to Dotty's jacket or top. A male gets a long-stemmed red rose in a plastic tube, as though he's bought it for his secretary or girlfriend. Then Dotty is given a card with the tiger symbol, onto which is printed her personal identification number and a phone number.

Dotty is given an empty canvas shopping bag, the kind you can buy at any Woolworths store, and she is told to walk to a second nearby location, which involves crossing a busy intersection that is usually filled with people. Somewhere on her way to this location and with a crowd of pedestrians around her, a Vietnam veteran, known as a 'Joe', will pass her and, without missing his stride, will drop a padded envelope into her shopping bag. The envelope, of course, contains a one-ounce phial of highly refined hash honey.

Dotty and her Smoky will readily recognise each other if she needs a future drop. Dotty can now use the phone number on her card to call a recorded voice, which asks her to wait and automatically dials another phone number. The second number gives a recorded female voice, very businesslike, which instructs her as follows:

After you hear the beep, give your account number and state the quantity required. Orders are restricted to a maximum of four, delivery in three days, usual contact time.

Though it might eventually be possible for the police to locate the whereabouts of the two phones they would not know how to pin down the twenty-five additional phone numbers these phones can dial up at random unless, of course, they got hold of the coded tape in the answerphone.

These random numbers belong to telephones placed in twenty-five separate homes belonging to the Vets from Hell bikie gang. The tape messages consist only of an identification number and a single-digit number up to four. In other words, no names, no pack drill, the caller cannot be identified. Each evening a call is made from a public phone box by one of the original Smoky Joe's mob to the owner of every phone and the numbers are taken down and translated into orders.

No system, of course, is perfect, but in the late seventies and early eighties it is a pretty sophisticated set-up.

Gazza, who is not only an electrician but has also spent time as a phone technician with PMG and was the radio operator in our platoon, has rigged up the two contact phones to a PMG terminal box in the street on the pavement outside Animal's house. A disused underground stormwater pipe runs along the side of the house and can be reached by climbing down a manhole situated in line with the backyard.

The pipe was discovered by Animal and his brothers and sisters when they were kids. 'We used it as a cubby house and when me old man come home drunk it were the only place we were safe from him,' Animal explained. 'We'd keep an old mattress and blankets down there to sleep the night and come out when it was safe in the mornin'.'

So if the police are able to locate the whereabouts of the terminal box, there would still be plenty of time to remove either the phones or the tapes in the answer-phones before they are found.

It proved to be a pretty good system, provided nobody talked.

Now you may be thinking, like we all did at first, that someone, take for instance Dotty Marche, wouldn't hand over the envelope with the hundred bucks in it in return for a red rose and a shopping bag. I mean, it's a bit bloody ridiculous when you think about it. You go up to this sheila you've never seen in your life before, she pins a red rose on you and gives you an empty shopping bag and tells you to walk to a certain spot where she'll be well out of your sight and, in return, you hand over a hundred bucks. Give me a break, will ya!

Wendy, though, was spot on again, she's relying on word of mouth among the social set to get her message across. The new client has been told what to expect by someone who she trusts and who has gone through the routine before. In other words, every new contact is a referral by someone the new client knows. It becomes a case of mutual trust. But, as almost never happens, if a potential client does refuse to hand over the money until she or he has got the dope, then the Smoky involved simply thanks them politely and walks away, the contact terminated.

The Smoky is always the same person for the client,

but the Joe, who makes the drop, is different, so he cannot be recognised and followed should the police set a trap.

The point is that if a Smoky is apprehended she is clean, she hasn't handled any dope. What's more, the Joe she is working with has to be caught in possession to be charged. This would require considerable luck, as a police ambush would be very bloody difficult to set up on an unknown and moving target. The Smoky never repeats the location of the hash honey drop. Even if they catch the Joe after the drop, he never carries more than one deal at a time and so he is also clean.

In fact the customers are the most vulnerable so it is in their interest to keep their mouths shut about their personal Smoky and pick-up arrangements.

Trenton le Gaye has spread the news through the gay community and White Tiger, as hash honey is now known, becomes the 'in' drug among the gays as well as the rich. It is this second market that will make the whole scam work.

Soon we are making money, big money, hand over fist and the love life of the yuppies, who were once the weekend hippies, the gays and the trendies has never been in better shape.

The hash honey is brought by Shorty to Smoky Joe's

Cafe, or I pick it up from the farm. Then half a dozen bikies from the Vets from Hell call into Smoky Joe's as though they've just stopped at a country cafe for a meal and drive it back to Sydney where it is decanted from one-gallon tins into single deals contained in one-ounce smoked-glass phials.

The money is now being used to make the lives of veterans' kids with spina bifida and other birth deformities a lot easier. Where corrective surgery can't be performed, wheelchairs are paid for, modifications made to bathrooms and toilets so that parents can cope with their severely disabled children. Most of this work is done by Vietnam vets tradesmen who are paid a salary.

The money is also being used to assist veterans who are ill and unable to work and for those needing counselling. Lawsy has set up a legal arm to take on the government. Nam Tran has a project to build a hospital in Vietnam for children. Most of this is done through a registered fund called Vietnam Veterans Self-Help Association that is run by Shorty.

Little Anna is now permanently in the Children's Hospital and not getting any better. Time is running out for us. On top of all this, the old cocky dies. In my opinion the world is a better place for her absence as she's well past her use-by date. But she's still Wendy's mum and she loves her and Wendy doesn't need any more personal grief in her life.

Wendy and I see almost nothing of each other these days as she is in Sydney full time, training and running the new Smokies and Joes and organising their schedule so it goes like clockwork. Meanwhile I'm keeping the cafe going in Currawong Creek and acting as a courier.

Lawsy manages the day-to-day operation. Wendy has her hands full and old Thommo has an empty bed for all but one weekend a month.

Once a month on a weekend, I get Brenda Hamill and her husband to run Smoky Joe's for me and I go down to Sydney to see Anna and, if I'm lucky, get a bit of a cuddle from Wendy who has R and R and is out of the civilian jungle for two days when Maureen takes over her job.

They've closed the books on Anna's chemo treatment and her hair is growing again. Anna's been bald from the chemotherapy that long that I almost can't remember how she looked with a head of hair. She's got her mum's hair and it's growing into a golden fluff on her little head. More than once I've broken down at night, wondering how long her hair will get before it's all over for my darling.

I try to persuade Wendy to sell Smoky Joe's so that we can be together in Sydney. I can't see Wendy coming back to running Smoky Joe's when this is all over. The hash honey scam is going so well that Shorty reckons we'll be through in less than a year.

'What then?' I say to Wendy. She knows what this means. It means Anna is no longer with us and the scam isn't there to take her mind off things and the two of us are together again.

'Thommo, this whole business will soon be over and if we're lucky enough not to be caught, then we'll need somewhere to go after this.' She sighs, 'I'm tired, it will be good to get back to Currawong Creek and away from all this.'

All Wendy's ever taken from the scam are her expenses and not a penny more. Lawsy wants her to get a weekly salary like the others, but she won't hear of it. She won't let me take nothing neither.

'We're fighting against an unfair system, Thommo,' Wendy says. 'It's us against Canberra. I'm doing this for Anna, *because* of Anna. She's going to die, we know that now, there's no chance of a bone-marrow transplant.' Wendy looks at me, still fighting back the tears. 'I don't want her little life to be for nothing. What we're doing is against the law and so I can't take any pay, that would make me a criminal.'

'What's the difference? If we're caught they'll treat us like criminals anyway. Shorty and Lawsy want you to go on a salary, it would help a lot, Wendy, we're slowly going broke.'

She sighs, 'No! No, Thommo, we'll manage somehow.'

I start to think how it would be if Wendy were caught, just Wendy in prison alone. I panic and want to throw up just thinking about it. There was once a bit of talk when we were all together on Shorty's farm about how, if one of us got caught and put away for a stretch, we'd mount an attack, a prison break-out. The platoon going in, rescuing our mate, like old times in Vietnam. It's all bullshit, of course, we've seen too many Yank movies, we're doing the John Wayne in our imaginations.

Maybe Shorty and Bongface and perhaps Nam Tran could still be effective warriors in a stoush with the prison guards, but the rest of us couldn't fight our way out of a wet paper bag.

Killer Kowolski and Animal look pretty macho riding on a Harley, but they couldn't run fifty feet without dropping dead. Macca's a physical and mental wreck and Ocker Barrett ain't that much better, both have the thousand-yard stare and they're suffering through more crook days than having good ones. Lawsy wouldn't have the stomach for it any more. Flow Murray would probably spill the beans down the pub the night before and, besides, he has a serious dose of the permanent shakes as well as the rashes and violent mood swings. I reckon he'll be the first of us mob to cark it. It's bloody amazing to me that we're holding the scam together at all and I wonder who's gunna break first among us, the majority of us are hitting the piss pretty hard. If it weren't for Shorty, Bongface, Nam Tran and the two girls, Wendy and Maureen, I reckon we'd be history. Lawsy's doing a good job, still thinking straight, but you can see he's only just holding himself together.

Despite all this, things drugwise continue to go great. Maybe God protects foolish old warriors? But as you can see, things are not all that good for the forward scout and yours truly. I love Wendy and our little daughter more than my life and the closer we get to the end of the whole business the more I'm shitting meself.

I try to imagine what would happen if Wendy and me were thrown into the clink and Anna was dying alone? Every day I wake up I can feel the panic in my gut growing bigger. The nightmares are worse than ever and the rashes are givin' me hell. I'm feeling butcher's most of the time. Even the once-a-month cuddle don't work no more. I've gone impotent again and I can't get it up to save me life. I reckon it's more the worry even than Agent Orange or post-traumatic syndrome. I even try hash honey, but it don't do no good and I'm feeling ratshit most of the time.

Then I start to think, even if we don't get caught, I'm gunna lose Wendy as well as Anna. I mean, why would a chick as good as Wendy want to stay with someone like me when the kid wasn't there to keep us together? With the talent she's got she could get a big-time job in the city. Her wanting to keep Smoky Joe's don't bring me much comfort neither. I tell myself it's just a sentimental thing, that she'll soon get jack of running a greasy spoon in a small country town and go back to the bright lights. What's happened to Anna is my fault and she's going to resent me and I don't blame her. What can a big, useless bastard like me offer her anyway? All I've ever done is make her life a heap of shit. If she left, that would be the end for me, shotgun in the mouth time. I don't reckon I would want to make it on me own. I'm feelin' that sorry for myself, I'm crying meself to sleep of a night.

So this is my state of mind when Shorty calls me.

'Thommo, can you get someone to look after Smoky Joe's this weekend, you're needed in Sydney?'

'What for? I'm not supposed to go down for another two weeks?' I know it can't be Anna because Wendy's phoned the night before.

'Mate, it's important, can't speak on the phone. Oh, and don't tell Wendy yer coming, okay? There's a good reason, trust me, Thommo.'

I finally agree and tell Brenda Hamill, who ain't that happy. She and her husband have planned to go down to the coast for the weekend. She knows things are tough for Wendy and me and, no doubt, she thinks it must be about little Anna, so being the beaut person she is, she don't ask questions and agrees they'll postpone their weekend and look after Smoky Joe's for us.

Shorty and Lawsy meet me at Sydney Airport and we take a taxi to Maureen's house. Naturally I'm worried, but they won't tell me nothing except that it's not a problem with Wendy or a crisis with little Anna. As we get closer to Maureen's house I think about Mo. I always do coming to her place. I still have a bit of trouble looking at Maureen, she's pretty and all that, but I can see Mo's eyes and his jawline and she has the same blazing red hair. Shorty and Lawsy hang back at the gate and I go ahead.

'Well, well, lookee who's here,' Maureen says when she opens the door. She turns and shouts back into the house, 'Wendy, someone for you!'

Wendy comes through into the hall, she must have been washing the dishes back in the kitchen because there's soap suds on the back of her left hand and she starts to wipe her hands on her apron. She's got no make-up on and is wearing jeans and one of my old shirts under the apron. One sleeve is half torn at the top and her rounded shoulder pops through the tear, the bottom of the shirt comes to well below the apron. She's that pretty my knees start to buckle. I can feel me heart going thump, thump, thump in me chest like it wants to jump right out and bounce across the floor so as to get to her first.

'Thommo!' she exclaims and I can see she's real happy to see me, surprised and happy, her blue eyes welcoming. She's coming up to kiss me and I've got me arms out to lift her up off her feet, when suddenly there's a helluva racket, a bloody great roar, then over it all a big road-train horn blasting, *BARP-BARP-BARP*! The roar grows and grows, filling the air so the windowpanes are rattling and I can feel the vibration through the soles of my shoes. Then *BARP-BARP-BARP* again and again and then it all stops dead except for several Harleys revving down and the sounds of people shouting out. Wendy looks past me. 'Oh my God!' she gasps, 'Oh my God, Thommo!'

Chapter Seven

I can hardly believe my eyes, not only are there maybe fifty members of the Vets from Hell on their Harleys outside Maureen's house, but also this red Kenworth truck has pulled up. It's not new but someone's done a damn good spray job. It's got a custom-built back on it which is also red duco and buffed to a high shine like an Arnott's biscuit van, only it's longer. There's an air conditioner unit on the top of the roof and what looks like a small electricity generator. On the side, in beautiful sign writing in white and gold letters, is written:

The Anna-mobile
Blood Testing Unit
Take a test & you could win $10,000!
A project of the Vietnam Veterans
Self-Help Association

The last of the big bikes rev their engines and then shut down and we see Shorty and Lawsy grinning and waving at us from the footpath.

'C'mon, over here!' Shorty yells.

I take Wendy's arm and I can feel her shaking. 'What the hell? What's going on?' I say as we reach the pavement.

People are clapping and yelling, the original Smoky Joe mob are now standing along the side of the big rig, Bongface has his smile on and the others all look very bloody pleased with themselves.

'Good on ya, Wendy! Thommo!' people are shouting.

We're grinning and saying gidday to the boys, not quite knowing the exact reason for the general merriment, but waiting for a proper explanation. To tell the truth, we're a bit embarrassed and a bit choked up at the same time.

Lawsy takes Wendy's arm, 'Want to take a look inside?' Wendy sniffs then nods.

'It's nice,' I say to Shorty, 'good rig.'

'It's ten years old, but it's been rebuilt from the chassis up,' he points to the bikies, 'The boys did it, built the back as well, sign writing, the lot. Mate, wait 'til you see the inside.'

We move around to the rear of the giant Kenworth.

There's a door open in the back and steps leading up into the van. Above the door it says 'Surgery', Wendy goes first, then me, followed by Shorty and Lawsy. Inside is a bloke about my age, maybe a little older, nuggetty build, short with bluish stubble even though he's close shaved, black Irish I reckon. He's wearing a white jacket and there's a stethoscope around his neck, so he must be either a nurse or doctor. Behind him are two women, also in white coats.

'This is Doctor Mike McGraw,' Lawsy says.

The bloke takes a step towards us and extends his hand to Wendy. 'Just Mike will do fine,' he says smiling.

'Wendy Thompson,' Wendy says, trying to smile. 'I'm sorry, I must look a mess. This is,' she gulps, 'well, a bit of a surprise.'

'A nice one, I hope,' Mike says, grinning.

Then he turns to me, 'You probably don't remember me, Thommo, but I was an Australian MO on duty at the US Hospital in Vung Tau when you came to see about your mate Mo Jacka after 6 RAR got back from the stoush at Long Tan?'

'Yeah, of course,' I say to him, shaking his hand, 'How ya goin', Doc.' I'm lying, I wouldn't have known him from a bar of soap, but it's not all that surprising.

After we'd pulled out of the rubber plantation and returned to the base I'd requested special permission to go to Vung Tau to see Mo. Sounds crazy now, but at the time I was paranoid, what with his head missing, that they wouldn't have him properly identified so that he could be sent home. I hadn't slept more than a couple of hours in the last twenty-four and I guess I was that rooted I wouldn't have noticed the doctor attending if he'd been Mr Magoo in a white coat.

Then Wendy and I are introduced to the two ladies, Sue and Marlene, one is a nurse and the other a lab technician. We are told they were both veterans' wives. What we don't know, and learn later, is that their partners are dead, the one from cancer while the other's gone and chopped himself. Vietnam has struck again. Sue turns out to be a highly qualified nurse and Marlene has a science degree and has worked for the Red Cross Blood Bank for nearly ten years.

Mike McGraw explains that the interior of the Kenworth is a complete surgery and at the back, in a separate room, there's a fully equipped laboratory. It's all been certified by the Health Authorities as a travelling laboratory. There's even a reception area for volunteer patients, where their medical history is taken down and their records kept.

'We're going to find an unrelated matching donor for Anna,' Shorty grins, 'even if we have to test every person in Australia.'

Now Wendy loses it completely, she can't stop crying and I'm pretty choked myself. I put my arms around her, 'I dunno what to say, mate,' I keep repeating, grinning like an ape and shaking me stupid head.

Eventually though, we pull ourselves together and Wendy says to Mike McGraw, 'It's such a very long shot, doctor, a million to one chance that we'll find a match-up.'

Mike nods, you can see he knows the odds, 'We'll never know if we don't try, Wendy.'

Shorty cuts in, 'Wendy, you helped make this all possible. Without you I don't think we would have gone very far. You'll be happy to know the business is over, Nam Tran says the bees have stopped buzzing and we're fresh out of honey.'

Lawsy laughs, 'In our case you could say we've had a very successful liquidation sale!'

Shorty continues, 'Our accumulated resources are going to help a lot of vets' children, veterans as well.' He waves his hand, indicating the surgery, 'One of the ways we'll do this is the Anna-mobile. We're going on the road, we'll find every Vietnam veteran we can throughout the country, check him out, check his kids out, talk to his partner. Get their stories and lobby the government, this time using our *own* medical records.'

He turns to Mike McGraw. 'Mike here has spent most of his time since coming back from Vietnam at the Prince of Wales Children's Hospital Cancer Unit. We've got all the gear we need right here. Can you show us the lab please, Marlene?'

We walk to the front of the van and Marlene opens the lab door. There's only room for two inside so she and Wendy go first and I stand at the door and look in. I must say it looks pretty impressive, not that I'd know what I'm looking at of course.

'The latest automatic serum dispenser, typing tray scoring system, oiler, the whole kit and kaboodle,' Shorty says behind me. You can hear the pride in his voice. 'We have the freezer unit and the facilities to do the basic tissue-typing tests right here. Then any samples that look like they could be a match have to go to Sydney for further analysis. Mike's got that process well in hand.'

Lawsy cuts in, 'You've seen the side panels, we'll offer a $10,000 reward for any member of the public who matches Anna's tissue type and is ultimately approved for a bone-marrow transplant.' He looks at Wendy and me, 'We know it's a long shot, but, well, we talked it over and the boys felt we had to give it a go.'

That night there's a big party held in the regular Vets from Hell's local pub in Bankstown, so the cops don't take too much notice. Everyone involved over the past year is invited, the pub is full to overflowing and I can't believe we've managed to keep the whole scam quiet for nearly a year. It's a real credit to the brother and sisterhood. Wendy says I have to make a bit of a speech to thank everyone for the Anna-mobile. I try to get her to do it, but she won't. 'It's your job, Thommo,' she insists.

I'm not much good at this sort of thing but I have a go, Wendy's standing beside me. I'm halfway through when I lose the plot. Then someone starts singing 'For they are jolly good fellows' and the mob take it up and I'm saved.

Wendy, Maureen and me get home after midnight. For once I'm not pissed. I want to stay sober to be with me wife all night. We end up in Maureen's kitchen having a bit of a late-night fry-up or, if you like, early breakfast, coffee, bacon and eggs. We eventually get to bed around three o'clock. It's been a bloody long day but it's amazing what good news can do for the cuddle factor.

Shorty and Lawsy have been to see everyone involved in the Smoky Joe scam and each participant receives an envelope with a nice little gratuity on top of what they've already earned over the past year. They are also told never to talk about their role in what's happened, that it's a Vietnam veterans' secret and must be kept that way.

Of course we're not in the absolute clear, we've got nearly a million dollars in cash that we can't explain if the Taxation Department come snooping around. Though Lawsy says there's 'ways and means' and he's in the process of applying to have the Vietnam Veterans Self-Help Association registered as a tax-free charity. He's pretty confident he'll get it through.

Any hopes I might have had of getting my wife back to a calm and settled life are soon dashed. Wendy is smart enough to realise that a thing like the Anna-mobile is not going to go unnoticed, that the media are going to see it as a big story and that we have to get all the ingredients right so that it can become an opportunity for having a go at the government. She talks to Shorty and he calls a meeting of the original Smoky Joe mob, plus Maureen. The only one missing is Nam Tran. Naturally we ask Shorty how come Nam Tran's not present? He says he'll explain later.

Shorty tells us how they've filled in Nam Tran's lab on the farm and dismantled and burned or trashed all the other bits 'n' pieces. He's back to rice, citrus and a bit of winemaking. Then he says, 'I've got a bit of a confession, it's about Nam Tran.' He stops and looks around at all of us. 'He's gone to the States.'

I guess we're all stunned. 'Why's that?' Macca asks eventually.

'He's going to try to do the same thing there.' Shorty clears his throat, 'Look, I haven't been entirely truthful about him, you see he's a doctor. I mean he was Viet Cong all right, that's true enough, but he was a surgeon in the North Vietnamese Army.'

'So why couldn't you tell us that?' Bongface asks, a bit aggro. 'What difference would it have made?'

'Well, that's just it, he had his own agenda. He wants to build a hospital in his own country to look after children affected by Agent Orange. I promised him one-third of what we made in return for his supplying the marijuana seed and his expertise with growing and refining the dope. We couldn't have done it without him. If he can do the same with the veterans in America, it's a much bigger market, he'll get all the money he's going to need.'

Lawsy stands up, 'Nam Tran's also given us a way

205

to launder the money, which means we're clean.' He doesn't explain any further, but goes on to say, 'We've been incredibly lucky with the scam, we got in and out in less than a year, not enough time for the drug squad to really get going. If we'd continued much longer, well, the chances are they'd have been onto us and we'd have been blown out of the water. Nam Tran's expertise, his hash honey, was the difference that made the difference.' He looks at Wendy, 'That and the way it was distributed and sold so that we caused no ancillary crime, kids never got hold of it and there was no harm done to the general community. In my opinion Nam Tran earned his share.'

There is complete silence in the room. I don't know what to think. Do I feel betrayed? Obviously Lawsy was in on it as well. Then I think to myself, 'Typical bloody army, they tell you just enough to get the job done but never the whole story.' Still, it looks like the battle is won. A man should probably punch Shorty out. Maybe I'm a weak bastard, but what with the Anna-mobile, I mean, what can I say? The whole thing stinks? No way!

To my surprise Wendy stands up and turns to face the mob. 'I know I feel a lot better having heard what Shorty has just said,' she blurts out. 'Kids are the same everywhere, they don't start the wars but they're usually its victims. I'm very glad we're helping Nam Tran's people.' She sits down next to me and I can feel her trembling. What she's just said I know I wouldn't have had the guts to say, even to me mates.

Then Maureen, who is sitting with Wendy and me in the front, turns around and says, 'When my brother Mo died in Vietnam I was pretty bitter. I asked myself a lot of questions I couldn't answer, and nobody seemed able to answer them for me. Why did Mo have to give his life for his country when his country shouldn't have been fighting the North Vietnamese people in the first place? When his country didn't care about him? So when Wendy asked me to help with the Smoky Joe scam I thought it was a way to fight back, to help Mo's mates and the forgotten and neglected warriors, to do something in Mo's memory.'

It's all come out so fast Maureen's hardly taken a breath. Then she says real quietly, 'But now there's something I can be proud of, we're helping our own children, helping ourselves to get better and we are helping the children of Vietnam. I feel good about that, Mo would too.'

We're all pretty choked, but Animal says, 'Jesus! I think I'm gunna throw up!'

The laughter this causes clears the air and I guess Shorty is almost forgiven for not spilling the beans on Nam Tran. After all, what can you expect from a bloody sergeant?

Shorty says Wendy's gunna talk to us. I touch her on the arm as she gets up, she's still the general and I'm the grunt, but I love her more than ever.

'Shorty has asked me to tell you about Anna's condition,' she starts, 'so you'll know what we're up against. You all know by now how Thommo and I feel about the Anna-mobile. We will never be able to repay your love, whatever the outcome. We thank you all for taking a blood test on Anna's behalf when you first knew about her. Now our greatest delight is that others will benefit as well, veterans' kids and vets themselves, that the Anna-mobile is not only for Anna.' She stops and takes a breath. 'I have to tell you that the chances of finding a bone-marrow match-up are very remote. You see, what's happened to our daughter is that she no longer has an immune system. That is, she no longer has any white blood cells to fight off infection. If we can find a matching donor, the bone marrow taken from the donor and infused into Anna could give her a new immune system, that is new white blood cells to fight off infection and so kill the leukaemia. Usually the donor comes from within the family and even this is rare enough. Finding an unrelated donor . . . well, we're going to have to be very, very lucky, one chance in a million lucky.'

'We've been lucky so far, maybe it will hold?' Bong-face calls out and there is a murmur of agreement from all present.

Wendy hasn't finished yet. 'Perhaps I can talk about another aspect of the Anna-mobile,' she now says, 'there's another opportunity here to publicise the veterans' cause, to get the Agent Orange message and everything else out to the public. That is, if we go about it in the right way. The Anna-mobile is going to attract a lot of publicity once we're on the road and it's up to us to make the most of it. We'll never get a better chance to bring up the issues involved and in the process try to shame the government into some sort of action.'

'What do you think we should do?' It's Ocker Barrett, who usually doesn't say much.

'First thing is to make it a spectacle, a big event when we come into town.'

'It's a pretty big rig, it ain't gunna go unnoticed when we pull into a small town,' Gazza says.

'Exactly right!' I say. I know where Wendy's heading and I can't help myself.

'You're right, but there's a lot more we can do.' Wendy points to Killer Kowolski and then to Animal, 'That's where your lot come in. If the Vets from Hell, the whole mob, move into a town or suburb as an escort for the Anna-mobile it's going to create quite a sensation. Then when we've parked in the town square, the bikes disperse and the vets give out leaflets to the good citizens, explaining why we're in town and urging people to have a blood test.'

Killer Kowolski doesn't let her finish. 'Jesus! One hundred and fifty Harleys, that would be really something.' It's not hard to see he's pretty excited at the prospect.

'Reckon you can organise that, Killer? Animal?' Shorty now asks. If them two still have a thing about Wendy, which I don't think they do, I reckon their differences are sure enough settled at this very moment.

'Oath,' Killer replies, 'The boys will be in on it in a flash.'

'Righto then, it's just a question of what town to choose for the launch, or should it be in Sydney?' Shorty asks Wendy.

'My first thought was that Sydney would be easy for the media, the obvious place for the TV channels. But the more I thought about it, the more I think it should be a small country town, somewhere near a bigger town, like a regional centre, so we can repeat the performance the next day and allow the media time to get there and turn the whole thing into a media event.'

Wendy must've seen by our faces that we were a bit confused. I mean, why make it hard for ourselves, when if we did it all in Sydney the media could stroll down the road so to speak and we'd make it happen big time first time up?

'So, why not in Sydney?' Spags Belgiovani asks. It's the obvious question for all of us.

'Well, it's up to us to decide, I suppose,' she adds quickly, 'The media will respond either way. It's just that I thought, you know, if we left Sydney and travelled through a number of towns to our destination, it wouldn't look like a deliberate media hype, a set-up? Though, of course, we'll make sure that our progress is reported so they see it as a possible news break.' When no one speaks she adds, 'We'll get more out of the story this way.' I can sense she's not certain she's right, that she'll back down if she's pressed and go for the city.

'Hey, Currawong Creek! That's where it all started!' We all turn around, surprised that Animal's had an idea. 'Well, why not?' he says again, 'It's where

Thommo and Wendy live, best fu . . . I mean, bloody good place to start.'

I'll never be certain that Wendy hadn't got Currawong Creek in her plans all along, but now Animal's said it, it seems like the obvious place to start, to park the Anna-mobile slap-bang in the middle of town outside Smoky Joe's Cafe.

The town has a population of nine hundred people and I reckon just about all of them would come in for a blood test. It'll be the biggest day in Currawong Creek since the pub burned down on the night after Don Bradman and Sid Barnes each made 234 in the Test match against England in 1946. The town loves Wendy and they've almost forgiven me for my earlier behaviour, though I suspect this is mostly because of Anna's illness.

If Wendy had hoped for a media scoop, none of us were ready for what was about to happen. We leave Sydney about four in the morning for the Riverina, it's about a seven-hour drive, maybe eight or nine with stops on the way. We aim to get to Griffith about lunch time, then on to Currawong Creek.

By the time we reach Wollongong, about eighty clicks out of Sydney, a regional TV crew are already onto us.

One hundred and fifty bikies on Harley-Davidsons and the big Kenworth Anna-mobile make an awesome sight tooling along the highway at sunrise, though we're careful not to break the speed limit or give the cops any reason to stop us. Goulburn is the next big town we pass through, horns blaring, *BARP-BARP-BARP*, down the main drag and out onto the highway again. We stop for petrol and Cokes, then on to Cootamundra and just on lunch time we come into Griffith.

Griffith around these parts is the big smoke, the regional capital of the Riverina. But after Sydney it looks small, a sort of going nowhere place. Then I think to myself, if Griffith looks like two chooks scratching around the shithouse, then what about Currawong Creek? It's a drop of passing bird shit splat on the bonnet of a ute.

Still and all, Wendy and me are coming home, it's like the circle is complete and we're doing something positive about our lives, about little Anna. We may not get what we're looking for, the chance of finding a tissue match for the little bugger is still a million to one, but we're in control this time and it feels okay. Matter of fact, it feels bloody marvellous. No more government, no more handouts and being thought of as bludgers working the system. We're helping ourselves, doing it our way and, as I said, it feels fucking wonderful. I'm driving the Kenworth on this last section, it's an old rig but a good 'un and whoever done the mechanics done a bloody good job, it's got a good donk, running smooth with plenty o' grunt.

I glance over at Wendy seated beside me, she's got her eyes closed, head resting against the window, having a bit of a kip I hope. She's lost a fair bit of weight and her jeans don't fit as snug, the crinkles 'round her eyes have deepened and there's a bit of a line starting to pull downwards from either side of her mouth. All these months she's never complained but I know she's taken a hiding, there's been a whole heap of shit she's never spoke about to anyone, just copped it sweet and said nothing. Being the forward scout in the civilian jungle has taken its toll, that and little Anna.

We're nearly into town and suddenly I've got this heaviness pushing up into my throat, it's like my heart wants to force its way out or something and then I feel the tears running down me cheeks. Jesus, how I love this little bird! I can hardly see the road for me tears and I hit the air brakes and Wendy jerks awake. 'What is it, Thommo?' she asks.

I want to tell her how much I love her, how much she means to me, she and the brat, how without her and the kid my life would be a piece of shit, but I don't trust myself to say it proper. 'Griffith' is all I manage to grunt.

She looks out the side window, 'Oh look, there's two helicopters following us,' she shouts.

The blokes from the regional TV station caught up with us when we stopped for petrol but all we told them was that we were headed for Griffith and then Currawong Creek, just to whet their appetite like, sort of invite them to come along but staying dead casual like it don't matter to us if they don't, it's no big deal. It must have worked because now there's two media helicopters following us.

'Channel 7 and Channel 9,' Wendy shouts. She's wound down the window and her head is sticking out, the wind sending her blonde hair streaming back, with the sun catching it and the rushing air tearing at her words. I guess the media have got the message all right, another bit of Wendy's organisational genius falls into place.

In Griffith, except for two sets of traffic lights, we don't stop. People, hearing the roar of the bikes, are running out of the shops, restaurants and pubs to see what the racket is all about and the helicopters follow us all the way to Currawong Creek, where we finally come to a halt outside Smoky Joe's Cafe.

BRYCE COURTENAY

The boys disperse on their bikes to hand out leaflets door-to-door. I don't have to tell you it works a treat, there's two national TV-station choppers landed on the showground.

The good burghers of Currawong Creek, the lame, the pissed and the sound of mind, to a man and his dog, they've all turned up and the queue stretches all the way from the exhibition shed to Willy McGregor's pub. With the thirsty citizenry and the bikies in town, Willy is doing such a roaring trade that he is reluctantly persuaded to send over a slab of beer for the workers.

Currawong Creek is finally on the map and for once it feels good to be a part of it all. People keep coming up, asking, 'Have you closed Smoky Joe's for keeps?' They seem pleased when we say we'll be back in a while. One old chook squints up at me, 'Can't say you've always behaved yerself, Thommo, though you're not the only one not done that in this town. But you're one of us, always have been, always will be, welcome home, son.' That was real nice.

Currawong Creek kind of sets the pattern we learn to use in other places, the Vets from Hell moving their big Harleys from door to door, passing out pamphlets, explaining the cause and inviting people to come on down and have a blood test. Of course there's the

216

incentive to win the money but most don't seem to care and say they'd come anyway. Country folk don't seem to have the hang-ups the city has about Vietnam.

Wendy and me and Shorty and Lawsy are on the box that night on national television. Wendy and Lawsy do most of the talking with her explaining how the Vietnam vets are sick of being pushed around and she tells about what's happening to our kids, then Anna's story and the reason for the Anna-mobile and how everyone's contributed to make it happen and to take responsibility for their own kind and stuff the effing government.

Well, the shit hits the fan big time and the story goes international and is picked up by NBC and CNN, the BBC and the French and German networks. There's the picture of little Anna in the isolation bubble with no hair from the chemo she's getting. Her story touches the hearts of people everywhere, particularly the Americans, who've got the same Vietnam guilt over the rejection of their vets as we've got.

Because Anna has no resistance to infection she has become what the hospital call 'a bubble child'. Which means she is placed in a large sealed and sterile glass enclosure where filtered air is pumped in. The hospital allow the media to photograph her and even for short periods to talk with her. She's got her mother's brains and is pretty bright and knows what's happening and is happy enough to talk to the reporters.

There was one famous occasion when this American female reporter from 'The Johnny Carson Show' asked her if she knew what the Anna-mobile was all about.

'Oh yes,' she exclaimed, 'They're looking for blood to make me better again.'

'Do you know what type of blood?' the reporter then asks.

Anna puts her head to one side and thinks for some time. 'Well, it has to be very red and it's a secret nobody knows 'cept the person who's got it.'

'And if they find this person, what then?'

Seven-year-old Anna looks at the reporter as though she must be stupid or something. 'Well, then her and me will share the secret and the person will get a lot of money and be very happy and I'll come alive again.' And then she adds the words that ring around the world, 'But you mustn't tell the government.'

'Why mustn't we?' the interviewer asks.

''Cause they don't like to help kids whose daddy went to the Vietnam war.'

Anna must have heard Wendy and me talking at

some time to have come up with this last bit, because we'd certainly never put it to her like that.

Anyway, this, and the Anna-mobile along with the Harleys and the Vets from Hell, interviews with small-town people standing patiently in long queues to have a blood test, all makes powerful television.

Wendy and me don't like exposing Anna to the media but the kid doesn't seem to mind and tells us she likes the television and people talking to her, though it's kept to an hour a day. I guess it must be pretty lonely living in a glass case an' all.

The hospital too is anxious to get the publicity as they are hopelessly underfunded for their leukaemia research and the State government has just cut their research budget in half. Two of their most brilliant young researchers are being forced to go to America to pursue their careers. The brain drain, so common these days, is on again and nobody in government, Federal or State, seems to care. Given the fact that little Anna's prognosis isn't real good we can't really object to the publicity opportunity they see in Anna. After all, they're doing all they can for our little daughter and the care she's getting doesn't come cheap, I guess it's a matter of you scratch my back and I'll scratch yours.

It would be nice to say we were getting somewhere

but so far we've done several thousand tests on the road without any luck. There's been nothing even remotely worth sending to Sydney for further analysis, not even a poor match to raise our hopes a little.

The American public goes apeshit about Anna and, of course, the treatment of their own vets and their children is brought up in the hullabaloo. Their veterans are not exactly backwards in coming forward and soon the whole Vietnam catastrophe is back in the news and back on the political agenda.

On the third week after the first exposure Anna receives eight thousand get-well cards from all over the world. The Minister for Health and the Prime Minister make statements, the usual bullshit, but no matter how hard they try to kill it, the story won't die. The world is looking in on Australia and not liking what they see.

The same is happening in America, we've lucked in, they're in the middle of the Presidential election and both the Republican and Democrat candidates make pronouncements, both promise they'll look into the Agent Orange issue the moment they get to the White House. The President promises he'll talk to Australia and politicians bring up the issue about Agent Orange in the House of Representatives. This is a festering sore in America's own backyard and Congress decides it's time they tackled it once and for all.

Naturally all this takes months and meanwhile we're out on the road doing blood tests in one small town after another. There is also money being sent from everywhere, particularly from Americans.

During this period a leading Sydney newspaper commissions a survey looking into the poor health of Vietnam veterans and their children in the Sydney area. The preliminary findings of the survey indicate a high incidence of suicide among Vietnam vets, general poor health, psychological disorders and, among their children, a rate of birth defects above the national averages. Though they are only preliminary findings they cannot be easily ignored.

The survey causes a further uproar and again makes the international news and the Americans start to ask the same questions of their own veterans. The *Washington Post* commissions a project in the District of Columbia with almost identical results.

The story stays alive long after the governments of both countries would have hoped it would die down. Here in Australia the Vietnam Veterans Self-Help Association demands a royal commission. Too many people are asking too many awkward questions and the government is forced to stop back-pedalling and do something constructive.

Meanwhile Shorty and Lawsy have become international spokesmen for our Vietnam vets. Wendy is in a league of her own. American women not only see her as a mother who is fighting for the life of her child, but as a feisty woman and a seeker after justice. She is someone who will fight for her man and all the other warriors who fought in Vietnam and still remain essentially herself. She is huge in America and her face appears on twenty different magazine covers, including *Time*. She's invited over to appear on 'The Johnny Carson Show' and naturally she won't leave Anna so they send over a crew to interview her, with Johnny Carson speaking to her on the telephone.

I'm dead worried about her, she's under a lot of pressure, we both are, but mostly Wendy, and, frankly, I don't know how she withstands it all. The little blonde is stronger than even I thought she was and that's saying something.

Okay, enough of that. I'm starting to feel sorry for the Thompsons and that's just not on. So, accept that when I tell you the whole thing is huge, larger than life, you've got to believe me. You may even remember it yourself.

But on the Anna front it's not the same good news. We keep plugging away day after day in all the little towns and the bigger country centres. Sometimes we stay at the pub, that is if there is one, sometimes we're invited into people's homes and sometimes it's sleeping bags on the side of the road and a cup of coffee brewed for breakfast in the hope that we'll hit a small town with a cafe for a bit of mid-morning tucker.

Travelling with the Vets from Hell also has its moments, the boys like a drink at the end of the day and with a gutful o' booze there are the inevitable fights. At first the local cop would be called in by the publican but this didn't always have the calming effect desired. What's more, to put thirty bikies in the slammer for the night takes a bit of doing even if there's more than one cop about. Even though the scrap might be between two blokes with nobody else taking much notice, the moment the fuzz arrive it's one in all in, the boys in blue have to arrest everyone or nobody and that's got its complications. There's not too many country lock-ups can take a big mob, mostly they're designed to accommodate half a dozen or so Abos drunk and disorderly of a Saturday night. What's more there's not too much enthusiasm for the task when it's all said and done.

Shorty and me soon learn that it's back to Vietnam with these buggers, they'll accept discipline from their own but not from outside. First thing we do when we come into a new town is visit the local constabulary and explain the situation and do the same to the local publican. Any fuss in the pub or anywhere else they're to call Shorty, Bongface or me. Generally speaking it works out okay but occasionally I cop a slap or two I don't care for and am obliged to settle the matter on the spot. I'm a big bugger and they soon learn I can give as good as I get and Bongface can give a lot better. On the other hand Shorty is still the sergeant and even a drunken bikie knows better than to molest him.

What we can never really get over is the kindness country folk show towards us, the biggest hearts are in the dusty little towns that don't seem to have a good reason for being where they are. I guess I should expect it, Currawong Creek ain't exactly a metropolis and there's a residue of kindness there I know I, for one, don't rightly deserve.

We'd come into some fleabag town on the Sturt Highway, the temperature in the mid-thirties, and the people would come out and line up and joke about themselves, how they're nobody from nowhere, and tell you about a kid from the town who went to Vietnam and how they're dead proud of him. Sooner or later he'd turn up, a vet wanting to talk to his own kind and it wouldn't be hard to tell that he was doing it rough like so many of us, hitting the booze or the pills or just being a loner. The town never put shit on him. Like the old bird in Currawong Creek said about me, he was one o' them for better or worse and he'd done his bit. Vietnam was never something to be ashamed about in the boonies. I guess a one-horse country town is no place for a weekend hippy or a protest march. Country folk know what kind of damage a war can do to a son or a father or even a grandfather, country women have been copping the effects of war on their men for three generations, from Gallipoli to Vietnam. It's not like the city, in the country everyone knows your business and when things get bad and the broken parts in your soul start to play havoc with your head and your heart, you can't hide the trauma in a suburban backyard shed.

Another thing that opened our eyes a fair bit in the bush was the way the Aboriginals hung out on the outskirts of the town, not really a part of it but the town dependent on their booze money and the shops selling them their tucker. Bongface once said to me, 'Thommo, they hate us, but they need us real bad, 'cause if we're not getting pissed and our gins are not there to show them what happens to a sheila when grog gets a hold of her, they'd have to look at themselves a whole lot closer.'

I guess it's easy enough to see virtue in country people, thinking they've got things in their hearts that city folk have lost, but there's a lot happening in the bush that's not good, attitudes and that which you wouldn't want to teach to your kids. It's not all sweetness and light by a long shot.

When we get into a town Bongface makes a point of rounding up all the Aboriginal kids and putting on the gloves and having a bit of a spar with the older ones. Then letting them put the gloves on and have a bit of a go at each other, meanwhile coaching them and at the same time laughing a lot and talking to them about being proud to be black. He then brings them into the Anna-mobile for a check-up. Most have something that needs to be done, boils to be lanced and treated, problems with their ears, partial deafness being a big thing with black kids. They're written up and their card sent to the local health officer so they can receive further treatment.

After the black kids come the adults, lining up, wanting to have a blood test because of Bongface. On more than one occasion this causes a bit of a ruckus among the white folk because there is this notion, not always without reason, that there's a lot of VD about among the blacks. How they think they're gunna catch it from standing next to an Aboriginal in a queue Christ only knows. Besides, it's not all that uncommon to find the same in a white bloke.

Generally speaking we're doing a fair bit of good. The Anna-mobile is doing a great job flushing out the Vietnam vets and their wives and kids. Mike McGraw is joined by two more doctors who served in Vietnam and, in most towns, the local doctor is grateful for the help and happy to cooperate with us. We're building a case to take to the government that can't be denied.

All this is well and good and a bloke feels a part of something half decent, the international media hasn't given up on us and most days we're good for a story, though not all of them are positive. They soon cotton on to the disparity between blacks and whites in the country towns and there's more than one story went out that wasn't going to do us any good nor is told with a totally fair perspective.

Racism is one of those things that brings out what Lawsy calls 'the vicarious instinct' in reporters which sort of means they try to find the ugly and the unusual and make it seem like it happens every day. Still there's a fair bit going on that's far from an exaggeration and we can only hope that things between black and white get a bit better in Australia and particularly in the bush.

After all, they're a part of us and we of them, no point carrying on like white is right and black is not, that's all bullshit anyway and don't do no good. There's as many white drunks in town as black, only the white blokes are better at hiding it, goin' home and beating up the missus in private instead of in public outside the pub like the black guy. Anyone with half a mind knows what's really going on.

Anna's time is running out. She's in remission but, with no T-cells to fight infection, the odds are that it'll be sooner rather than later that, even in the bubble, she'll catch something that will take her away from us. Even if she doesn't the doctors say that in the end the leukaemia will get her. Sometimes when we're camping out and I'm lying on the side of the road looking up at the stars I can't help thinking that the Big Boss up there doesn't give a shit.

Wendy now only leaves Anna's side to take part in media conferences, all of which take place in the hospital so that she's never far from our daughter. Like I said, I'm with the rig but whenever possible I go down to Sydney on the weekends. With Smoky Joe's closed for the duration, Lawsy fixed it so that the Vietnam Vets

Self-Help Association, which is now a registered charity, supports us. The hundreds of thousands of dollars that have been sent to Anna from all over the world have gone into the charity and Lawsy says, if we'd wanted to, we could have kept it all ourselves, so it's only fair. Though we're forced to accept it, Wendy and me don't like it one bit. No bastard wants to appear to be bludging. But, the truth be known, there's bugger all we can do, there's nothing in the bank and Wendy doesn't want me to sell Smoky Joe's. Not that a country cafe in a one-horse town would fetch much anyway.

It's nearly six months since we started on the road and still nothing. It all looks so bloody hopeless. If it wasn't for the bit of good we're doing, I reckon I'd chuck the whole thing in. I've got this monster dose of the shits and I'm feeling right sorry for meself and seriously thinking of giving up when we pull into a tiny little town named Daintree, near Port Douglas in Queensland. There's not a lot different about this place, a bit greener with rainforest and a nice beach with a few surfers and hippies about, bludging, on the dole no doubt. It's what Lawsy calls a place in the sun for shady people. Shit, why should I care, good on 'em, my kid's gunna die, she's never going to crack a wave, bludge on the dole, feel the warm tropical sun on her back, salt on her skin. What's more, my own health isn't all that grand neither and I'm worried, Wendy doesn't need a big useless bastard like me about, she's that bright she proved she could make it on her own. I know how loyal she is and that's getting to me as well. I'm scared she'll stick with me and in the process fuck up her own life. I've seen what's happened to some of the vets we've met on our travels, the human wrecks, grog, drugs, you name it, they're fucked and they're not coming back, you can see it in their eyes, they're living somewhere else. It's like seeing me own future. I'm sitting on a rock looking out at the ocean, gulls careening above me, hoping for a free feed while I'm thinking all this shit. 'Better give it away, Thommo, time to go, mate,' I say aloud. 'When Anna goes do the deed, hey.' I tell myself Wendy will be grieving for her daughter, best to double up, so she can get it over with as quickly as possible.

'Hey there, Thommo!' It's Bongface come up back of me. 'How ya been then?' he asks. 'Nice day, hey?'

He must have sensed something because then he shuts up and comes to sit down beside me and is real quiet for a while, the both of us looking out at the ocean, young blokes on their surfboards, sun shining on wet shoulders. Then he lights two fags and hands me one and we smoke, looking and saying nothing. After a long while he says, 'Met someone today, reckons you and her are related.'

I don't bite and it's silence between us again.

Then, after a while, 'She saw yer ugly mug on the box, reckons you're a dead ringer for her father, only you're a whitefella.'

'She one of your mob then?' I say, not too interested.

'Yeah, but she's got your name, Mona Thompson.'

I take a drag and exhale and look at him squiffy-eyed through the cigarette smoke, 'So? It ain't exactly the world's most unusual name.'

'True, but that's not all. She give me this picture, photograph.' Bongface laughs, 'I could have been lookin' at you, only darker complexion.' He looks at me again, this time I can see he's dead serious, 'Thommo, it *was* fuckin' you! I'm tellin' ya, mate.'

My heart begins to beat faster. Now I remember, Mona is a name used in our family from way back. I don't want to hope, but I can't help myself. 'My great-grandfather's brother went walkabout with an Aboriginal woman not long after they arrived in Currawong Creek.' I look at Bongface. 'Couldn't be, though, that was before the First World War.'

Bongface shakes his head, 'Can't say, might be,

231

might not, who knows?' He flicks the butt end of the fag onto the sand below us. 'All I know is, I took her in to see Marlene in the Anna-mobile to take a test. Marlene says it's the best yet, a damn good match, though, of course, she can't be positive until the blood sample goes to Sydney for further analysis.'

I grab him by the shoulders and shake him, 'Mate, what are you saying?'

Bongface smiles the Bongface smile, 'I think maybe we've got her. We've got the bastard!'

Epilogue

It is Anzac Day and I'm at the dawn service at the Cenotaph in Martin Place, Sydney, and I'm crying. It's a good place to cry because there are others doing the same, older women and old-timers from earlier wars. I'm just the latest crying recruit, one of the younger ones crying for Vietnam. Crying for what it's done to our lives. I'm clutching the little Vietnamese doll and wearing the medals Thommo never wore.

I can't say our life with Dad was easy, far from it, Vietnam saw to that. But what I can say is that Mum and I were loved every day of our lives. No matter what happened, we knew that big old cranky bear loved us.

Sometimes during my childhood Thommo would lock himself up in the bedroom and I'd ask Mum why. 'He's fighting the ghosts of the past,' she'd say. Once when I put my ear to the door I could hear him crying. The only time

I actually saw him weep was when I was seven, not that long after I'd had the bone-marrow transplant, when he heard that Shorty had incurable cancer. 'He knew all along! He knew all along!' he kept saying over and over.

Five months ago, at the ripe old age of fifty-four, Thommo was also diagnosed with cancer of the bowel. The Ghost of Vietnam had come to claim another good man.

During the last few weeks of his life Mum and I would visit Thommo in Concord Hospital every day. Then one day, when he seemed a bit better than usual, he said to me, 'Baby, get one o' them tape recorders, bring it with you next time you come. I've got one more thing to do before I die. Bring lots of tapes, you hear? A man wouldn't want to run out in the middle of his tale now, would he?'

Almost every day he'd give me a completed tape, though some days he was too weak to talk. 'Sorry, love,' he'd whisper, 'I'm too crook to talk into that thing, I must be getting old.' The nurses said the tapes kept him alive weeks after his time was well and truly up. 'It's your story I'm telling, darling, I want you to know what happened, what a clever mum you've got,' he told me on one occasion.

Then on the fifth of September he gave me the last

tape. 'The bastard's done!' he whispered, typical Thommo. He was terribly ill and only just able to talk, my big old dad, so thin you could see the veins and the shape of his bones through his almost translucent skin.

On his arm was a tattoo of a gun. 'What's "Mo" mean?' I'd ask as a child, seeing the writing on the butt. He would always give me the same answer, 'It's just one of those stupid things young blokes do.' Then, when he handed me the tape, he held my hand a long while. My big, beautiful dad was so frail I could barely feel his grip. His words, when they came, were painfully slow, 'Anna, on Anzac Day I want you to go to the War Memorial in Hyde Park and find Mo's name on the wall, tell him you're Thommo's daughter, introduce yourself.'

My father died in the early hours of the following morning with Mum holding his hand. I've transcribed his story just the way he told it on the tape.

The sun has just risen on a lovely early autumn day, shining down on us through the long, cold grey canyon made by the tall buildings on either side of Martin Place. A lone bugler is playing the Last Post. It's for Thommo and Mo and all the other brave warriors of Vietnam, telling them we remember.

Anna Thompson, Anzac Day, 2000

Glossary

AK47   automatic assault rifle used by Viet Cong and North Vietnamese Army

APC   armoured personnel carrier

B52   high-altitude bomber

Charlie   Vietnamese soldier, derived from Victor Charlie or VC; used to denote the enemy

deep j   deep jungle

DLP   Democratic Labor Party

dustoff   helicopter used to evacuate the wounded and dead from the battlefield

Geographicals   veterans who cannot reside in one place for long

grunt   popular nickname for infantryman, adopted from American army usage

H & I   harassment and interdiction – artillery fire at irregular intervals targeting suspected enemy supply

routes and assembly areas
hutchie   one-man shelter, tent
M16   automatic rifle used by Australians and
Americans
MO   Medical Officer
nasho   National Serviceman called up for
compulsory National Military Service
Noggies, Nogs   name for all Vietnamese, used mostly
for the enemy
NVA   North Vietnamese Army
OC   Officer commanding a company of soldiers
Owen gun, Owen machine gun   sub-machine gun used
by Australians, largely replaced by the M16 by 1968
Post-Traumatic Stress Disorder   psychological
problems caused by major traumatic incidents, in this
case the Vietnam war
provost   military police
R and R   rest and recreation, leave in another country
RAR   Royal Australian Regiment
R in C   rest within the combat country
RSL   Returned Services League, established in
Australia in 1916 to provide assistance to those who
served in the armed forces and their dependants
SLR   self-loading rifle used by Australians
VC   Viet Cong

THE AUSTRALIAN TRILOGY
THE POTATO FACTORY

Ikey Solomon and his partner in crime, Mary Abacus, make the harsh journey from thriving nineteenth-century London to the convict settlement of Van Diemen's Land. In the backstreets and dives of Hobart Town, Mary builds The Potato Factory, where she plans a new future. But her ambitions are threatened by Ikey's wife, Hannah, her old enemy. As each woman sets out to destroy the other, the families are brought to the edge of disaster.

TOMMO & HAWK

Brutally kidnapped and separated in childhood, Tommo and Hawk are reunited in Hobart Town. Together they escape their troubled pasts and set off on a journey into manhood. From whale hunting in the Pacific to the Maori wars in New Zealand, from the Rocks in Sydney to the miners' riots at the goldfields, Tommo and Hawk must learn each other's strengths and weaknesses in order to survive.

SOLOMON'S SONG

When Mary Abacus dies, she leaves her business empire in the hands of the warring Solomon family. Hawk Solomon is determined to bring together both sides of the tribe – but it is the new generation who must fight to change the future. Solomons are pitted against Solomons as the families are locked in a bitter struggle that crosses battlefields and continents to reach a powerful conclusion.

JESSICA

Jessica is based on the inspiring true story of a young girl's fight for justice against tremendous odds. A tomboy, Jessica is the pride of her father, as they work together on the struggling family farm. One quiet day, the peace of the bush is devastated by a terrible murder. Only Jessica is able to save the killer from the lynch mob – but will justice prevail in the courts?

Nine months later, a baby is born . . . with Jessica determined to guard the secret of the father's identity. The rivalry of Jessica and her beautiful sister for the love of the same man will echo throughout their lives – until finally the truth must be told.

Set in a harsh Australian bush against the outbreak of World War I, this novel is heartbreaking in its innocence, and shattering in its brutality.